Woman in Blue

DOUGLAS BRUTON

Fairlight Books

First published by Fairlight Books 2025

Fairlight Books
Summertown Pavilion, 18–24 Middle Way, Oxford, OX2 7LG

A CIP catalogue record for this book is available from the
British Library.

1 2 3 4 5 6 7 8 9 10

ISBN 978-1-914148-68-2

www.fairlightbooks.com

Printed and bound in the Czech Republic

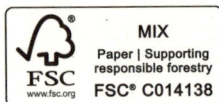

MIX
Paper | Supporting
responsible forestry
FSC
www.fsc.org
FSC® C014138

To MF

Prelude

This never happens. Almost never. He wakes in the mid-night and the not-yet-morning and he wakes with a picture in his head. It is not the waking that never happens, for some nights the urgent weight of his bladder pulls him from sleep. Especially so on guild nights when he has drunk too much ale – there's a cloth-covered beaten copper chamber pot beneath his bed for just such an eventuality. But it is not his bladder that has disturbed his sleep this night. It is the picture in his head that has woken him.

'Do pictures speak?' he wonders. 'Do they shout loud as cattle drovers?' For how else has the picture banished sleep? He can see it complete and finished, like a jewel, everything lit up blue and gold – all the colours of a day in summer. That's how he sees it on waking. And there's a woman in the picture and she is not aware that she is seen. There is something about the woman, he thinks. Something he recognises. At least it feels like recognition.

He opens his eyes on the darkness in the room. He listens, his ears sharp as dressmakers' pins. He hears nothing at first, then the slow and heavy breath of his wife beside him in the bed; he hears the spaces between her breaths the loudest. Catharina is in the first months of her pregnancy. He hears the unfaltering ticking of the clock in the hall and the house shifting as houses do, the small cracks and clicks, the dance steps of tables and chairs. Maybe it is one o'clock or two; he would have to get out of bed to check on the time.

He turns in the bed, turns his back to his wife, who is asleep. He closes his eyes and the picture is before him again and the woman too; he sees that the woman is young and she is dressed in blue. She's pretty, he thinks – but then aren't all young women pretty to a man whose wife is pregnant and all out of shape and distant? The young woman's hair is pinned up so he can see the gentle arc of her neck as she bends her head a little. He can see the clasp in her hair, the ribbons on the sleeves of her dress – is it a dress or a jacket she wears? She is reading a letter that she holds up to the light. Her lips are parted as though in reading she is also giving silent shape to the words.

It is an idea for a picture. That's what he thinks. Perhaps it should be his next painting. He makes a note to himself to sketch out the picture in the morning. Then he looks again for sleep.

But he is unsettled. He knows enough about thoughts and ideas to understand that they are sometimes as fleeting and gossamer-thin as breath. He knows that when the bells of the Nieuwe Kerk ring out across the city to announce it is morning, all memory of the young woman wearing blue will have evaporated in the rush and run of things – the fire to be seen to, the children to dress, his wife asking him to make a decision about some small domestic matter of no consequence. And the woman in blue presses her demands on his attention now.

'Who is she?' he thinks. 'Why does she exert such a pull on me? Is she someone I once knew, long before? Does she have a name? What is the letter she is reading?'

He opens his eyes again. He must get up and make some record of the picture. He knows doing that at least will fix it so that he can conjure it entire in his thoughts when he wakes again. He pushes back the bedcovers and swings his stockinged feet to the floor. He sits a moment, his eyes adjusting to the darkness. Then he pushes himself up from the bed, careful not to shake the wooden frame and wake his sleeping wife.

The air is chill and he sucks in breath, tastes metal or blood on his tongue.

He creeps from the bedroom, makes his way downstairs to the fire. There's still a warm glow to be found in the coals if you look. He lights a thin taper and transfers the flame to a candle. Then back up the stairs to his studio. He sets the candle down on the table and takes up a fresh sheet of paper and a stick of chalk. He closes his eyes a moment to better see her – the woman in blue reading a letter. Then he fixes his attention on the act of sketching.

His hand moves easily across the paper, each line certain and sure and quick. It is to him as though the picture already exists on the page and all he is doing is revealing it, letting the light fall on her and on the letter she is reading. It takes him almost no time at all – or it takes him an hour that feels like no time. He is a little giddy and a little breathless from the work.

When he is done, he drops the chalk to the floor and, without looking at the drawing, takes up the candle again. He returns to his bed, snuffs out the candle flame and slips back under the covers. Catharina stirs. He holds his breath until he is sure she has settled and fallen deeper into sleep. He rests his head on the pillow and thinks again of the young woman in the picture.

'It will be my best painting yet,' he says to himself.

But he also knows that all middle-of-the-night ideas seem brilliant when considered in the dark between sleeping and waking – those same ideas in the cold light of day less so.

And the young woman in his picture – already he thinks of the painting as 'his' – who might she be? That he does not yet know.

Delft, early 1663

A Man in Amsterdam

i

I know exactly where she is. I have a season ticket and I have been often to see her. I know the number of steps from here to there, but I am never in a hurry to get to her. Sometimes I approach her as though I do not know, as though this is my first time and I might walk right on by without ever noticing her. Then at the last moment, the last tiptoe step, I turn; I like that I catch her unawares.

She does not look up or in any other way show that she is observed. I am the one who catches my breath, for each time I see her it is a surprise. She is a young woman dressed in a blue bedjacket and she is reading a letter, all her attention fixed on the single sheet of paper she holds. We see her in profile. Her mouth is a little open as though she might be giving shape to the words she is reading. It is a private moment and yet we get to see it, to linger over it.

Sometimes it is a 'we' and sometimes it is just me. I come early some days. The man on the door knows me. He nods a good morning and lets me in. The floor beneath my feet is hard and my shoes click with every step. I take the stairs, not wasting time with the lift. But even then, I slow my pace as I come close, lightening my step so that there is almost no sound in the gallery, for I am the first. Then it is just the Woman in Blue and me, and I come upon her as though I have turned a corner in a house and seen her through an open door.

That, I think, is what the artist wanted the viewer to experience. There is something almost transgressive in watching her. I want her to lift her head and catch me looking at her and then to scold me with a hard stare as she clutches her letter fast to her bosom, all the words pressed to her heart and all the words secret again. Of course, this does not ever happen.

There is light in the painting and it falls on her, a soft blue-white light. A kind light. Indeed, at first glance it almost seems that the light emanates from her and behind me everything else is darkness, as though I might be standing in a windowless corridor on the threshold of the room where she stands in brightness.

Behind her, on the wall – on her wall – hangs a large map. It is painted in soft ochres and is almost golden and her hair is the same muted gold and so, standing in front of the map, she almost dissolves into the picture.

I do not speak. I sometimes hold my breath and like that it is as though I am in the picture too, as though I am nothing but pigment and oil and spirit – brushstrokes. But I am not alone with her for long. A woman with grey in her hair stands beside me, so close we touch, and she lifts her phone to the painting, frames the picture she will take and clicks; her phone makes the slowed-down sound that old cameras used to make. She smells too much of lemons, this woman beside me.

We are standing in the Gallery of Honour at the Rijksmuseum in Amsterdam. At the furthest end is the space built specially to house Rembrandt's imposing *The Night Watch*. But it is Vermeer's unprepossessing *Woman in Blue Reading a Letter* that has caught our attention and holds us charmed – holds this woman who smells of lemons and me.

You don't need to shout to be heard is what the painting seems to say.

The air has a controlled and even temperature and no one speaks except in whispers – like in a library or a church.

The woman beside me lifts her phone to the painting again, not trusting that she has taken a good photograph of it the first time. She would like me to move a little to one side, but she does not ask. Instead, she takes the photograph crooked. Then, without a second thought, she moves on to the next painting in the room and it is just me and the Woman in Blue again.

What I like about the painting – one of the many things I like – is how cleverly the artist has included me in it and made me complicit in the looking. It is an intimate and private moment and Vermeer intrudes on it without at all breaking it, and we – Vermeer and me – stand silent, breath held, just looking at this young woman turned in on herself. She does not know.

I have bought a season ticket to the Rijksmuseum, but that is a secret I keep to myself, the ticket folded and tucked into a small, seldom-used pocket at the back of my wallet. Most especially I do not tell my wife of the purchase, not over our good-morning break-fasts or our how-was-your-day dinners. I do not tell her because we are not really talking these days, at least not about things that matter. Or perhaps I do not tell her because it is something I want for myself and it is something I think she will not understand; when all's said and done, I do not understand it myself.

As for my particular interest in *Woman in Blue Reading a Letter*, I think that is also probably best kept hidden.

Woman in Blue

i

He loves me.

He thinks I don't know him, but I know. He approaches on soft slippered feet, as though he might be a daylight thief. He comes creeping and he thinks I don't know he is coming. Heartbeats make a sound if you have sharp enough ears, thumping as loud as any drum sometimes, and I hear his heart beating. Slow at first and then a little faster as he comes nearer to where I am. He has been here every day for the last week and sometimes so early he is the only one there. And he thinks I don't know him.

He looks as though he is walking from one end of the gallery to the other, but then as he comes level with me he turns to face me. It is something sharp as a pin, this sudden spin on the ball of his foot that he does. I can hear the rush of blood through him, the rub of leather against marble, the sole of his shoe against the hard floor. Then he snatches for breath.

I do not look up from the letter I am reading – I do not ever look up – and so he thinks I do not know he is there watching me. He keeps a distance between us at first. His lips are parted, like

men's lips when they kiss, like women's lips when they expect
to be kissed. He thinks he is playing a game, thinks he comes
upon me by some chance and that what he does in just looking
is something blissfully wrong, but looking is what I want him
to do.

Maybe it is what I wanted from Meneer Johannes Reijniersz
all those years ago. He came upon me just the same, turning on
his toes in Delft's Nieuwe Kerk and seeing me full in the light
dropping down from the stained-glass windows above us. Maybe
I let my gaze fall on him, just for a moment. My lips were parted
and my hair was combed neat and pinned back from my face and I
had nipped my cheeks so there was some colour in them. I wanted
him to look and he looked. His heart beat so fast I could hear it
under the thick velvet of his tunic, and he snatched for breath, too.

Were his fingers, even then, stained with blue?

I had heard he was an artist and so I had set my heart on him
noticing me and maybe asking to paint me. I did not have the
money to commission him to do so. All I had was my face. I'd
heard men say I was pretty and so I thought this might be enough
to win the heart of Meneer Johannes Reijniersz and that he would
one day ask me to sit for him in his studio. And this he did. Not
at first, not on that first day in the Nieuwe Kerk; a church is no
fit place for such business. But I made sure he saw me again some
days later in the street. He was caught off guard then, and all his
thoughts were flung and frighted birds in the air, and for a moment
he did not know where he was or even who he was – all that he
betrayed in the look on his face.

'Breathe,' I said to him quietly.

Then he remembered himself and a little awkwardly tipped his
hat to me and, finding his words again, he wished me a mumbled
good morning. He moved away from me then, but I already knew
it had begun and that it would all fall out just as I'd planned it.

I told only Katrijn, and like that it was *our* plan. 'He would pay good money to paint me,' I told her. Katrijn, whose hands were chapped and pink from so much work, who was up to her elbows in hot soapy water for hours some days, scrubbing the burnt fat and dirt from cooking pots, scraping dried egg from the rims of china plates and washing the coffee rings from the insides of cups, who worked long hours in a grand house for small money. My mother was a seamstress and sometimes she was a lacemaker when there was a lady to pay for such work, but her late mother – my grandmother – was a washerwoman and by that my mother understood how to care for sore hands; she said Katrijn should rub wool grease into her fingers at night and she showed me how to apply this home-made ointment and, after, how to wrap up Katrijn's hands in soft cotton bandages. Like that it was as though Katrijn slept with gloves or mittens on, and when she woke, she said all night she had felt as though she was being nudged on all sides by gentle sheep in a wide field.

I pointed Meneer Johannes Reijniersz out to Katrijn when I saw him one day at the fish market. She knew the plan by then. She nodded approval of my choice and laughed like a small girl. I think it drew the artist's attention to me once again. He blushed, perhaps realising that we were talking about him and that Katrijn's laughter was for him only.

He loves me and he thinks I don't know, but I know men.

A Man in Amsterdam

ii

After so many visits to the one painting – for I do not spend time with any other painting in the gallery but look only at the Woman in Blue – you'd think by now I would know everything there is to know about her. But each visit throws up something new. There's a low rope to keep you back from the painting, but that only governs the feet, for the body can tip forwards, leaning close enough you can almost breathe in the dry paint. Of course, if you are judged to be too close, a gallery attendant will let you know with the gentlest of admonitions.

Today, leaning into the painting, I notice the way the young woman's hair is pinned up so that, with her head bent over the letter she reads, her neck is bare and her hair falls in clotted curls onto one cheek. I knew someone once and when her hair did this, fell across her cheek, she'd reach up and with the most poetic movement of one finger she'd catch her hair, drag it back from her face and tuck it behind her ear. I couldn't help thinking that the action of her hand was practised, like writing, something she did without knowing she did it, or at least without understanding the simple complexity of what she did. It was also something so achingly beautiful that I wanted to loosen her hair and watch her do it all over again.

The woman in the painting also has a decorative clasp of some sort in her hair. No matter how close I am to the painting I cannot quite see the detail of this clasp. It is as though the artist gives us only his impression of it, as though he does not want us to get too close – getting too close does not sharpen the image. Too close and all you can see is paint and how smooth it is, so smooth that the brushstrokes aren't even visible.

I lean back a little and I can see the clasp again. It is the same colour as the map behind the woman's head and is only a little lighter than her hair.

'She's beautiful, isn't she?'

The man beside me spends maybe two minutes with the painting, makes this small observation to no one in particular and then moves on to the next painting in the gallery.

I am somewhat cross at this interruption. It has somehow spoiled the moment – after all, it is still early morning and I am used to being alone with the Woman in Blue at this time. So I retrace my steps to the entrance to the gallery, turn as though I am entering it for the first time that day, take a deep breath and come to the painting again. I perform the same casual approach and spin on my toes once I am level with the painting, coming to her as I always do, as if by chance, and my breath is taken away again.

On one side of the picture, the artist has put a dark wooden chair. We know this chair from other paintings by the same artist. He must have owned a set of these chairs. There are two of them in this picture. The chairs are upholstered in a blue cloth pinned down with brass-headed studs that pick up the light and quietly give it back again; this chair, pushed to the front of the picture, stands between me and the young woman. On the other side, a draped and indeterminate dark cloth hides part of the plain dress or skirt she wears. This darkness is for balance and along with the front chair is also to keep the viewer at a distance.

Sometimes I am here at the Rijksmuseum when it closes, when the smartly dressed attendant says in a quiet, almost apologetic voice, 'Excuse me, sir, but it is time for you to go.'

Time – it has run away from me, or stayed hidden, lost in a moment, lost in the moment of looking which is somehow something outside time. And now the attendant has brought me back with his 'Excuse me, sir.' I nod to him and reluctantly pull myself away, retracing my steps back through the gallery to the stairs down to the main entrance of the museum where the man on the door who much earlier let me in now lets me out again and wishes me '*goedenavond*' – good evening.

I do not go back to the apartment right away. Sometimes I sit in the small ornamental garden situated at the back of the museum. It is quiet there, save for the watery music of a fountain and the quiet chatter of a lingering child with its mother. And in this place, so quiet and so close to the Rijksmuseum, it is as though we are still together – the Woman in Blue and I.

Woman in Blue

ii

He loves me not.

He is looking only at my hair today, and he frowns when he looks. There is a pinched crease in his brow and it almost feels like he disapproves of something. Then he brightens. He is thinking about something else. Remembering. Someone he once knew, not me. His features soften and his eyes lose focus so that I am for a moment not even there in his vision.

I do not clear my throat pointedly or gently stamp my foot or in any other way show my concern at his not being with me then – except that under my breath, as though I am merely reading a script written for me on the piece of paper I hold, I say, 'Look at me. Look at me.'

Meneer Johannes Reijniersz was sometimes the same with me.

'I should like to paint you,' he said one day when we met. His words came out in a rush as though if held back a little they would not come at all. He was dressed in his Sunday clothes and I flattered myself that he had dressed so for me, for this accidental meeting in the street. 'I should like to paint you, if I may.'

I have no doubt that he thought this was a decision he had made – this man who was ever slow to make a decision. I am sure he thought he was the one who had decided I should model for him and that all he'd needed was the courage to ask. The truth was a little different. That was everything I'd expected of him, just as I'd told Katrijn. 'He will pay me just to sit and look pretty, you'll see,' I told her. In the end, getting him to ask me to model for him had been an easy first step.

He handed me a folded slip of paper and a small coin, then turned on his heel and walked away, but only as far as a shop doorway, from where he observed me reading the note. I do not think he meant for me to know that. I unfolded the paper and held it to the light to read his words. He had written down his address and a date and a time. All very formal, except at the bottom of the page he had written that I should wear my hair pinned up so my neck was bare. It was such an intimate detail that I think I might have blushed or smiled to myself – though in truth, if I did, that was all for him, for I knew he was watching.

I refolded the paper and slipped it into the pocket of my dress, along with the small money he had given. Then I crossed the road and entered the church to pray, even though there were no words to give shape to any prayer, no words and nothing more than the scattered thoughts in my head that I hoped God might make some sense of.

He was not the first gentleman to give me attention. My mother had warned me against encouraging men in fine clothes by smiling at them or looking at them with soft eyes. My mother dressed in clothes all the colours of darkness and kept to the shadows, testament to her creed that going through this life unnoticed was the way. 'There is safety in being so unseen,' she said. My mother was concerned for her soul – concerned too for mine.

Katrijn laughed when my mother said this about being unseen, not because she thought my mother's words foolish but because she knew the truth in them, thought the truth so plain and self-evident that she considered it unnecessary for it to be put into so many words. Since coming to stay with us, Katrijn had been an ally for my mother with her talk of what un-gentlemen might do to a pretty young woman.

And what does it mean when an artist says he wants to paint you? It means only that he has seen something in you that will serve his purpose. Nothing more.

If I didn't keep the appointment he had made, it would be of no more consequence to him than a wasted silver stuiver. He would find another woman to sit for him. And if I did sit for Meneer Johannes Reijniersz, then what? May a young woman sit for an artist and still be considered good and upright? Would the money he paid me – for there would be more money to be made – be enough to serve some purpose? All of this I spoke of with God. And I sat patient and quiet in Delft's Nieuwe Kerk, waiting for God's answer.

When I stepped out onto the street after praying, Meneer Johannes Reijniersz was gone. I took out the folded slip of paper and reread the words at the bottom of the page.

Later, I showed Katrijn what he had written. Katrijn does not yet know words that are penned so I read his words out to her, my finger following under the writing so she could learn. Then I held my hair up so she could see my neck just as he wanted to see it. That was how he wanted to paint me, nothing but that.

He loves me not.

A Man in Amsterdam

iii

It is a strange jacket that she wears, on top of a white undergarment that is visible at the neck. I read somewhere that it was a *beddejak*, a bedjacket, something only worn by wealthy women in bed. It hides all shape of her, makes her look heavier than she is, bell-shaped. The jacket is fastened up the front with blue ribbons and one that is a golden yellow. The sleeves are what might be called three-quarter sleeves and end just below the elbow. We see another piece of gold ribbon there.

The bedjacket is blue like the bluest sky and the yellow ribbons are like pieces of the sun. Is it fanciful to think this? I read in a reputable art journal that the bedjacket originally had a fur trim on the hem but the artist changed his mind on this and so everything is a great deal plainer, simpler. No fancy distractions, so that all attention is fixed on the reading of the letter.

The bedjacket gives us to think that it is morning and the young woman has just risen from her bed to take receipt of the letter. Or perhaps she is rereading a letter that arrived the day before, the week before. There is what looks like a second letter open on the table in front of her. Maybe she had been sleeping and dreaming and she woke a little disturbed by her dreams and she is rereading her letters to find her footing again.

It is a quiet painting – no bells ring. It is quiet not just because the young woman is reading, but quiet in its colours. There are no shouting bright orange carpets or loud lemon-yellow bodices or flaming red dresses that scream. Everything is muted. Even the yellow-gold ribbons are dulled so they do not unnecessarily excite the eye. But it is the blue of her bedjacket that determines the quiet, a blue that is echoed in the upholstery of the chairs and in both the light and the shadows falling on the wall and in the blue-black rod fixed to the bottom of the map behind the woman.

From somewhere to my left, the gallery attendant clears his throat. I am perhaps a little too close to the painting for his liking. I step back and almost collide with a woman standing behind me. Then I am suddenly aware that there is a small crowd gathered in front of the painting, all of them hushed as though in prayer. That is what the painting can do – what the blue in the painting can do.

The blue is a holy blue, someone once said, like something a Renaissance Madonna would wear as she holds her child close. It is this blue that elevates the young woman. Maybe we are supposed to think the blue bell shape of her is to do with a pregnancy. I also read that somewhere. There is some sense of the swelling of a woman with child in how Vermeer has painted her, in the way the artist has shown the blue bedjacket wrapped around her belly.

I lean into the picture again, listening more than looking. But everything is still and quiet; I hear nothing, not even the rustling of the folded paper she holds in her hands, not even her quiet breath, for we are in a still, blue moment and everything is caught and held.

After I have left the Rijksmuseum and the man at the door has quietly tucked his 'goedenavond' into the palm of my hand, pressed my fingers closed over it, I make my way along the Spiegelgracht. There's a café there and I like the tea they serve and the cups they serve it in: thin-lipped bone china cups. They serve coffee in paper cups too, and sandwiches wrapped in waxed paper – sliced brie on a bed of torn rocket leaves, topped with walnut halves dribbled over with honey. Most people take their sandwiches to go. There are only three small tables squeezed into the back of the shop – I like that too. It is quiet there, and sitting at one of the tables you cannot see out of the café onto the street, cannot see the passers-by, and so there is no distraction and all your thoughts are turned inwards. I sit in the almost perfect peace of this café and think about the day I have spent with the Woman in Blue, holding a little tighter to her, putting off the moment of leaving her and returning to my quiet wife.

Woman in Blue

iii

He loves me.

He thinks the blue of the bedjacket is something holy and he prays before me. At least, that's what it feels like when he leans into me. I notice that he is wearing a blue shirt today and I think that is maybe something he has planned so that he is somehow a part of the painting too. He is quiet also – but then he is always quiet. I sometimes want him to speak, to interrupt the reading of the letter in my hands, to tell me what he is thinking.

Of course, I know what he is thinking, but thoughts put into words have a different weight to them, a different colour.

I know there was a young woman in his thoughts once, when he was looking at my hair. His eyes took on a faraway look then, and there was a slackness to his mouth. It was as though he was transported to another place and another time and it was someone else he was looking at. The same look was briefly there today, when he was marking the yellow ribbon fastenings of my bedjacket. I wanted to look at him then, to bring him back to me with the blue of my gaze – I think a gaze may be blue even when the eyes are not.

When I called at the house of Meneer Johannes Reijniersz as arranged, the door was answered by a young girl who introduced herself as Maria. She was maybe nine or ten and had, I thought, more of her mother in her than her father. She said I was expected. She let me in, closed the door behind me. Then, taking my hand in hers, she led me up the stairs to the second floor of the house where Meneer Johannes Reijniersz had his studio. She knocked and then pushed at the door, but would not enter. I understood that was a rule for all of the family.

Meneer Johannes Reijniersz got up from a chair and introduced himself formally to me. I gave him my name and he said it back to me, over and over – like a litany prayer maybe, or as though he was testing the bite of a gold coin to assess its authenticity. He took my jacket – which was not blue – and draped it over the back of the chair he had been sitting in. Then he asked me to stand beside the table and in front of the two windows that streamed in yellow light. He gave me a book to read and then he stood back, as far away from me as he could get in the studio space. And all he did was look.

The book was a collection of psalms. It fell open at Psalm 23. The words on the page danced so I could not focus on them, even though it was a psalm I knew well. It was something my mother was fond of repeating. The words 'goodness' and 'love' kept rising to the surface as if in competition with each other. And time shifted.

Then Meneer Johannes Reijniersz was beside me and touching my hair, arranging it so that it brushed my cheek, and he was so close I could feel his warm breath on the back of my neck. Earlier, when the day was still candlelit and Katrijn was dressing for work, I'd asked her to help me pin up my hair so my neck was bare. I made comment on her ungloved hands and how they smelled of sweet grass and the sour breath of ewes. As she leaned into me I felt her breath on my neck the same as his.

'You may call me Johannes,' he said in a whisper.

I may have nodded.

He went behind a curtain and brought forth a piece of clothing. It was a blue jacket. He said it was the sort of jacket that women sometimes wore in bed. I did not tell him that I had never worn such a jacket to bed and nor had my mother or any other woman I was acquainted with. He asked if I could put it on, gestured for me to go behind the curtain for some privacy.

When I re-entered the room, he had arranged a thick, bright-coloured Persian carpet on the floor and added some cushions. He said I was to lie down in the jacket as though I was in bed. Then he lay down beside me and pulled a cloak over us.

'I want the jacket a little less shop-bought and a little more slept in,' he said by way of explanation.

Then he rolled onto his side and he laid one arm across me, not heavily but lightly, holding me as he would a gentle wife. And like that the morning passed. I do not think he slept and nor did I. The bells of the Nieuwe Kerk rang out the hours and the half hours, and each time it did so I was a little surprised that we had been lying together for so long.

When the morning was ended, he pulled back the cloak, got to his feet and said I should change out of the jacket now, gesturing again for me to go behind the curtain.

When I was dressed in my own clothes and came back into the room, our little bed was tidied away. Meneer Johannes Reijniersz – Johannes – took the blue bedjacket from me, pressed two silver stuivers into my palm and said I should come again the next day and that maybe we would start the painting then.

I may have nodded again, for besides gifting him my name I do not recall any other word I said on that first morning.

I stopped in at the church on my way home and prayed some more, and the substance of my prayers was all on my lying abed with Meneer Johannes Reijniersz. As innocent as it had been – for, hand on my heart, nothing indecent happened – I nevertheless felt the need to tell someone, to confess, and I judged God was as good an ear as any other. Telling God meant I did not have to tell my mother, with her finger-wagging admonishments against what men in fine clothes might do to a young woman's reputation. Indeed, telling God meant I did not have to tell anyone else, not even Katrijn, who knew the plan and might have understood that there was nothing in what we had done.

The churchman saw me sitting alone and approached to ask if I needed his counsel. The midday sun falling in through the windows threw the churchman into shadow so I could not see his face and his voice was soft as dream-talk and like that it was as though God was speaking. I thanked him for his kindness and assured him I was no longer troubled.

Then I was left alone again; the air was lit up and clean, and the quiet was stony and like a stopped breath. I could not help what I did then: I held myself clasped in my own embrace and – may God forgive me – I imagined it was Meneer Johannes Reijniersz who held me in his arms.

He loves me.

A Man in Amsterdam

iv

Sometimes I go to the gallery later in the day. Something blue in the city has perhaps distracted me. There is a shop near to the Rijksmuseum on the Nieuwe Spiegelstraat – Kramer, I think it is called – and in its windows are hundreds of antique blue Delft tiles. They have been carefully removed from the walls of old houses and now fetch a high price. I stop at these windows some days. The background of these tiles was, I think, once white but is now a step away from white. This is the result of age. But it is the blue that gives the tiles their name – blue lions, blue windmills, blue tulips. That blue is still blue.

When I arrive later at the gallery, there is always the risk that there will be more people gathered around the Woman in Blue – it's a different experience altogether from arriving early. I approach her then from the other end of the hall, stopping to look at Rembrandt's *The Jewish Bride*. This is a painting quite unlike *Woman in Blue Reading a Letter*. It shows a man embracing a woman. It should be another quiet and private moment, but it is something else; it is loud and brassy, the colours and the paint laid on so thick it is almost as if the young bride lives and breathes and could step down from the painting. You can hear the rustle of her stiff petticoats and her fiery-red dress, the jangle of her heavy bracelets; her breath you can hear too. The man in the picture is dressed in gold that almost blinds and the whole painting is a bold illumination that cries out of the coffee-spilled darkness of the background. There is just too much noise in the painting for me. I move quickly on to my Woman in Blue, and the quiet then is almost deafening.

She reminds me of someone, this Woman in Blue – I think I have had that thought before. She reminds me of a young woman I knew when I was young. I seem to recall once seeing her reading a letter, or maybe it was a book, but reading just the same as the Woman in Blue, except that her lips moved a little as she read and the air around her fluttered and the light danced. It is different in the picture, for there nothing moves. And watching the Woman in Blue reading her letter it is as though I stop existing and am just the pared-back pure act of looking. Then I both want her to move and at the same time do not want the stillness to be broken. This, I think, brings a tension to the picture.

There is a low seat in the gallery, not quite in front of the painting but near enough that the picture can still be seen – if there are not too many people in front of the Woman in Blue. I sit there some afternoons and just hold her in my thoughts and in my gaze. I do not know what it is exactly that I am looking for or what it is I hope to get from spending so much time with this painting.

'Don't you just love her?' says a woman sitting beside me.

'Sorry?'

'I have seen you here before just looking at the painting, looking at the *Woman in Blue Reading a Letter*. There is something remarkable in her. I sense that you see that. It's easy to love her, I think.'

I feel caught out, as though I have been seen doing something I shouldn't. 'I do not think "love" is the right word,' I say. 'I just enjoy the quiet the painting has.'

'Yes, the quiet,' the woman says. 'A momentary quiet.' She gets to her feet and moves away.

Maybe tomorrow I will not come.

On my way home I stop in at the shop selling blue Delft tiles. The light in the shop is thin and the air is dry and my breath tastes of dust. I once smelled the pages of an old library book – something musty, with vanilla notes and a faint taste of dark chocolate. The air in the shop is the same.

The man at the counter says he is sorry but they are closing in five minutes. He does not look sorry. He looks a little annoyed, the features of his face drawn into a rat-like scowl. He taps at the watch on his wrist. 'Five minutes,' he repeats.

I say I want only to purchase one of his old blue Delft tiles. 'I saw it this morning in the window,' I say. 'It has blue tulips on it.'

I do not know if this pleases the man at all. He sucks in air, holds it in his cheeks and then lets it go again. He pulls open a drawer from which he lifts a bell-jangling set of keys. Then he comes from behind the counter and asks me which window I saw the tile in. He unlocks the inner shutter and asks me to point to the tile I want.

When he lifts the tile up for me to see, confirming that it is the one I want, I sense a reluctance on his part to sell it to me.

'They are very old, these tiles,' he says. 'They are not so many now. They are a part of us, or a small part of us is in them.'

The tile was once white but is yellowed now with age, and a grey layer of dust has settled on the surface. Maybe the blue was once a little brighter, too. The back of the tile is marked with old plaster or cement, scraped roughly flat. It was once on the wall of a house outside of Amsterdam. 'An old farmhouse,' is what the man says. He wraps it in several layers of pink tissue paper, then in a sheet of old newspaper. Finally, he slips it into a used plastic carrier bag and lays it lightly down on the flat counter.

It is more expensive than I bargained for.

'It is a present perhaps?' he says, checking his watch.

'For my wife,' I say.

'Good, good. Well, we are closing now. Thank you.'

And with that he ushers me unceremoniously from the shop and locks the door behind me.

Passing the window I saw the tile in this morning, I can see there is now an empty space where the blue tulip tile was. I almost want to put it back, and maybe I understand now the man's reluctance in selling it to me.

And something else I understand too: that things belong in their own time and space and taking them out of that time changes everything. I loved a young woman once, but that does not belong to now – and the Woman in Blue belongs to another time entirely. And yet they also, somehow, come together in me.

A present for my wife, I say to myself and I turn to go, leaving the window of Kramer's changed, and clutching – out of its own time and space – a small blue tulip Delft tile in my two hands.

Woman in Blue

iv

He loves me not.

He says it is only the quiet he likes. Every day for almost a month he has come to see me, and now he says it is the quiet he comes for. And he says tomorrow he might not come. No thought about me in that. No thought about how I might feel, having grown so used to him looking at me each day and tomorrow suddenly finding him not there. He loves me not.

But it is no matter, for I am never alone for long these days. There will be someone else today after he has gone and someone else tomorrow and the day after. Always now there is someone. Yesterday there was a woman dressed in furs with a pearl necklace hanging about her neck, pearls that caught the light and then gave it back. She was, I think, struck by my appearance just the same as he sometimes is. She leaned into me in the same way and made to touch me with just the tips of her fingers, as though she did not quite believe her eyes.

The attendant was quick to stop her, and kind he was, too. He understood, for he once did the same and had to stop himself.

So, it is no matter that *he* may not come tomorrow. And yet...

Meneer Johannes Reijniersz said the same, about the quiet.

'Having so big a family and in so small a house, it is not easy to just be and not easy to enjoy the quiet even if it can be found. Here in the studio it is different. Here in the studio I can have all the quiet I need – a secret quiet.'

I turned that 'secret' over and over on my tongue, tasting what it might be. I thought of what we had done that first day in his studio – I thought of it often but did not speak of it, not with my mother nor even with Katrijn. Only God knew and He never would tell; He kept all my secrets. I remembered how Meneer Johannes Reijniersz and I had lain together for a whole morning, like a man lies with his wife, not talking, just being, and I remembered how he held me.

I dressed in his blue bedjacket at the start of each session. It smelled lived-in by this time. It smelled of my sweat, something sweet and thick like milk when it is boiled in a pan. I had taken to dabbing rosewater on the back of my neck before I came to the studio, a mask to hide the scent of me. The jacket smelled faintly of that too.

'And it is in your hair,' Katrijn said when she pinned my hair up before going off to work in a gentleman's kitchen. 'Roses in your hair.'

And it was on Katrijn's hands, so that the lady of the house where she worked, not knowing it was Katrijn who smelled now of rosewater, remarked on the scent of roses faintly adrift on the air. 'It is a summer smell, roses and new-cut grass and ewes with their lambs,' she said, and she imagined it was something that had been carried on the wind from somewhere far off, a place where it was always summer and there were always swallows throwing outsize geometry against the blue sky. The thought made the lady of the house smile, and she carried that smile through the rest of that day and into the next. And I think this made Katrijn smile too.

Some days Johannes – I called him Johannes only when I thought of him – was so quiet it was as though I was alone. He said that was the feeling he wanted in the picture and so he was glad I felt that. But there were times between posing, when we rested from the work we were about, and he talked then, and all his words came tumbling out of his mouth as though he had only this short interval in which to say everything he had to say.

The blue pigment, he told me, was a hard and brittle rock that he had to grind so fine it was softer than talc. He showed me. He called it lapis and he said it came from one place in the world and once it had been weight-for-weight more expensive than tulip bulbs or gold, so expensive that the pigment could be used only for painting the most holy, only for the Madonna herself. The place where the rock was mined was a far-off place, he said, where the air was so dry it sucked, so hot it scalded and blistered the tongue with every breath, and the people there ran around without clothes and had the heads of dogs.

I thought he teased me sometimes, and so I did not ever believe a thing he told me.

Then he was quiet and painting again and I was alone and with my own thoughts.

He paid me for each session. I kept the money wrapped in a handkerchief and hidden under my pillow at home. I dropped peppermint oil onto the handkerchief; my mother had once prescribed peppermint as an aid to sleep, but I did this to hide the smell of the money. They commonly say of men in fine clothes that they are stinking rich, and so I thought it must be their money that smelled. And the money – my money, wrapped in a peppermint-handkerchief – did begin to amount to something, and with such peppermint-money I no longer could think myself poor.

He told me to look as though I was reading. The paper he had given me to hold was blank, and so I told him it was hard to do that when there were no words on the page. He nodded and said he would do something about that for next time.

When he was tired or when the Nieuwe Kerk chimed for the middle of the day, he put away his brushes and he announced that he was finished and that I was too. 'For today,' he added in case I thought not to come the next day. Then I changed out of the blue bedjacket and into my own clothes. The quiet then was different, but it was still quiet. Sometimes there were no further words spoken and he did not even escort me to the door or see me down the stairs. It was as though I was nothing when he was finished painting for the day. Sometimes it felt that way.

On my way out of the house I once saw his wife. She smiled at me, but it was not really like a smile at all. She was expecting another child and so she was all swollen up and pink-cheeked, and she was, when we met, out of breath from sweeping the floor of the kitchen. I wondered then if it was for her just like it was for me, if when Meneer Johannes Reijniersz was done with her – as when he was done with painting for the day – then she was as nothing to him. I wondered if that was why he had lain down with me on that first day in his studio, and I was a little perplexed that he had not done so again.

He loves me not.

A Man in Amsterdam

v

I don't know why, but I have started removing my wedding ring before my visits to the Woman in Blue. I do not think it pays to read into these things. I have sometimes wanted to remove my shoes too, as you do when you enter the house of a friend whose carpets are the colour of oats or apple blossom or snow.

Today I notice how delicately she holds the letter in her hands. Maybe the artist chose her for the cleanness of her tapered fingers, so pale and so pretty. Looking at her fingers delicately holding the letter, I do not think she is a woman who could be pregnant.

And the letter, what does it say? It must say something to occasion such a concentrated reading; this is a question we are meant to ask. Her reading does not look feigned – which may be the skill of the artist, or perhaps it's that she really is reading something – but what might be written to hold her attention so completely? The artist does not tell us. At least not in so many words. That is what great art does: it allows the viewer in and the viewer brings something new to the painting, something of their own story and life and love.

I imagine then that she is reading something I have written to her. Maybe it is a love letter and that is why I have removed my wedding ring. I give her a name, this Woman in Blue, and once it is given I do not know where the name has come from.

Dearest Lieke,

Then the words I am writing to her just spin in the air and do not hold together. If words could be just feelings then *dizzy* and *love* and *yearning* would be those quietly spinning words and the letter would write itself. But *Dearest Lieke* is all I have. And that is what the Woman in Blue reads over and over, *Dearest Lieke, Dearest Lieke,* her lips parted like a small breath or even a kiss-in-waiting – and reading those words, she looks for something else in what I have written, some sense or connection. Maybe she makes as much as can be made from that *Dearest*, for it is the only word that has any meaning at all.

Of course, all of this is just a momentary fancy and is not really a part of the painting at all. The thoughts of the Woman in Blue are altogether simpler and quieter.

Afterwards, when I have left the gallery and replaced the wedding ring on my finger, then I think about what I might have written in a letter to Lieke. The quiet words come easily then. Not just one letter but enough for two – and thinking about that I remember that there is also an unfolded page on the table in the painting, as though she is reading both of my letters to her.

The man at the door thinks I am smiling at him when I leave the museum, and he wishes me a good afternoon.

Later, I catch myself saying her name over and over under my breath, the name I have given to her even though it does not feel like something given when I say it: Lieke. And I wonder then if it is a real name and if it has any significance.

I repeat her name sitting at dinner in the evening, saying it quietly to myself, quiet like a grace-prayer. My wife remarks on it, asks me what it is I am saying. I tell her it is nothing, just thinking out loud.

'Thinking about what?' she says.

'Something I am working on,' I tell her, checking my fingers under the table to make sure I am again wearing my wedding ring.

My wife is used to me not talking about my work – my writing – and so she does not press her enquiry any further. We talk instead about the weather and about what we can see from the window of our apartment – the lights in the street and the stars already winking in the night sky. My wife remarks that the inky blue of the sky is the same blue as the tulips on the Delft tile I gave her.

'Yes, something the same,' I say.

And like that the name of Lieke is lost or quietly hidden.

Afterwards, when I make a record of the day in my notebook, I notice that the name 'Lieke' starts with a 'lie'.

Woman in Blue

v

He loves me.

Lately he has taken to not wearing his wedding ring. He thinks I don't notice just because he does not see me looking up from the letter I am reading. The ring is in his left trouser pocket. I know this. There is a shiny band on his finger where the ring has left its mark on the skin, soft and pink like mother-of-pearl; that is something he cannot hide: that a ring belongs there.

And he writes me letters now. In his head he does and he thinks that because his thoughts are so quiet, they are secret and only known to him. Ha!

He loves me.

Meneer Johannes Reijniersz wrote me letters also. He said it was so I had something to read, something to concentrate my attention, and just so I looked the way he wanted me to look for the painting. 'Quiet letters,' he called them, by which I understood they were for me only and something close to secret. They were also bold letters – bolder than Meneer Johannes Reijniersz ever could be.

Dearest Angelieke,

I so look forward to your visits to my studio. It is the quietest time in my day and also the loudest, for my heart beats so hard – surely you can hear it? I watch from the window for your coming and I am a little fearful that today you will not come. But then you are there and the day suddenly has sun in it.

And the studio when you enter no more smells of oil and alcohol and candle grease but is awash with roses. When you have changed into the blue bedjacket and you have picked up the letter you are to read – this letter – then I sort the pose, fussing over the folds of your skirt so they are the same today as they were yesterday and all the days before. And your hair, I make sure it lies across your cheek as it should and I lean into you a little more than is necessary, breathing in the smell of you and the smell of roses too.

And I remember that first day in the studio when we lay down together on a makeshift bed and I held you as a man holds a wife and we slept together, innocent and under the watchful gaze of God himself.

Then I fall to painting and I lose myself in what I am doing and I lose myself in you. Is that possible, do you think? That a man can be so overwhelmed. And your lips when you are reading my letter, I watch them so closely that I think I see my words there and so I write here 'I love you', but just so that when you read these words it will be as though you are saying them to me.

If I am a little slow with the work – more deliberate and more careful – it is only because I do not want this

liaison to end. For what will be left of this when the
painting is done? It will sell soon enough, of that I have
no doubt, and then I will have nothing but the memory of
this time with you and I will find myself alone and bereft.
And seeing you across the market square or kneeling in
church, I will be heartsore.

Please one day do call me 'Johannes' and call me 'love'
and call me yours.

Johannes

Each day a new letter and a new declaration of love – a man
does not have to *say* he loves for there to *be* love. And when the
morning was spent and he had added a little more to the painting,
he took the letter from me and I went behind the curtain to change
back into my clothes – to become me again. Then I heard him
tearing the letter into a hundred pieces. It had served its purpose,
after all.

I told my mother and Katrijn about Meneer Johannes
Reijniersz's letters – not about the concealed declarations of love,
just generally about the writing and the having something new to
read each day when I was standing in the light from the window
with his gaze fixed on me. I did not think my mother or Katrijn
would care to know that a gentleman had told me he loved me,
that he had put down in inky words how he felt, the writing a little
scratched and uneven so even as I read what he had penned I could
hear a breathlessness in his words.

My mother looked up from her sewing, held the needle sus-
pended in the air. 'What on earth can he find to write about each
new-blessed day?' my mother said.

I shrugged and hoped by that to make little of it.

Katrijn looked at me and her look was all questions. Maybe
she had a better understanding of the things a gentleman might

say to a pretty young woman even if, had I one of his letters to show her, she could not read what Meneer Johannes Reijniersz wrote to me.

My mother had not yet returned to her sewing; her needle and thread remained as before, as though she was sitting for a painting and the artist had instructed her to hold the pose. I understood from this that she considered her question not yet answered.

'Nothing of meaning or consequence,' I said. 'Just words and so little in them that I never can afterwards recall what he has written. Something about his family, perhaps, and most especially his wife. And about the smell of the paint and the oil in his studio and each morning how the picture is progressing. And how the light is changing from day to day. And what he had for his breakfast and what he will have for his lunch when I am gone. And the price of bread these days and how he must purchase more candles and butter and chopped wood for the stove, and I don't doubt but a hundred other small details of his ordinary day.'

Words sometimes betray us, I think. It would perhaps have been better had I said fewer of them, for saying so many only betrayed me more.

Katrijn averted her gaze from me. 'Like a moth that is caught and pinned to a board, its wings spread wide so it is always obscenely on show – I think that is what it must be like to be looked at so hard,' she said then.

Later, I lingered over the application of wool grease to Katrijn's hands.

'It is just a letter,' I told her. 'Something to pass the time. Something and nothing, but mostly nothing.'

It was just a letter and at the same time it was something more. And I do not know or care if a man may be condemned for the thoughts that he keeps hidden or for words that he tears up into tatters. Meneer Johannes Reijniersz would say before anyone and before God that it was not love he felt – he was married after all – but God and I know.

He loves me.

A Man in Amsterdam

vi

I did not go to the gallery today. But that is not to say I did not think of the Woman in Blue. I have a postcard of the painting which I keep beside my bed. My wife asked me why it was there and I said it was my favourite of Vermeer's paintings. She said, 'Well, of course it is – it's the sexiest of his paintings.'

I do not know why she said that or if she really does think it is a sexy painting. It is not something that I have thought. Indeed, sex is not something I associate with the artist's work. Even *The Procuress* with its overtly sexual subject matter is just too pretty a picture to be sexual; not even the man's hand on the clothed breast of the woman as he drops a coin into her open palm speaks to me of sex.

No, as I have said before, there is something altogether cleaner in this painting of the Woman in Blue, something almost holy. When I look at all those Renaissance Madonnas in their blue shawls and their blue dresses, I do not see anything more or less than a woman – so when I say there is something holy in Vermeer's *Woman in Blue Reading a Letter* I am not really speaking of God but of something else. Something to do with respect and innocence and restraint.

And so I do not think of it as a sexy picture.

There is a map on the wall behind the woman. It is a map the artist has used before in the background of at least two other paintings. Its importance is up for debate. Some think it speaks to the inner world of the Woman in Blue and that she is thinking of a lover or husband who is absent, who is perhaps at sea on business. Maybe it is this man at sea who has written the letter she reads and because she is in her blue bedjacket we are meant to think that her first waking thought is for this man.

Personally, I think such a reading of the painting makes less of it than it is and does not really say enough to explain the impact the painting has on the viewer. I think the artist is better than this explanation would suggest. He has stripped the painting back to something simpler and yet altogether more complex, something universal. He has caught a mood in the choice of colours and how they harmonise with each other. And the woman holds the viewer, not because she is beautiful or even alluring, but just because she is.

If the painting could be simply explained then we would merely nod, acknowledging the craft of the artist, and then we'd move on to the next painting and the next again. But we don't. We linger. We take the time. We spend that time in her company and do not want to move out of it.

No, there is something more in this painting, and something that is not easily explained by the absence of a man.

I did not go to the gallery today. Instead, I took one of the tourist canal cruises – not for the commentary with its talk of a city built on land reclaimed from the sea and its mercantile history that once made it the richest in all the world; not to see the houses and to hear about the narrow staircases, so narrow that beds and sofas must be raised on hoists still visible on the outsides of buildings, everything lifted and then pushed through the windows into rooms that do not want for space or light; not to be told about the riddle of the house signs cut in stone above the doors of the buildings to say where once there was a butcher, a wine merchant, a trader in beaver furs; not to learn about defence towers and clocks chiming all out of time and out of tune. No, I took the canal cruise because at some point I knew that we would shift away from the city and out into deeper water that tastes salt-stung and clean. There all my thoughts could briefly disappear – up where the gulls scream and are not heard – and when my thoughts returned, as I knew they would, they'd be scoured clean and feel new.

When we returned to where the canal cruise started, I thought again of the Woman in Blue and she was then something pure and innocent and good.

When I am home again I am aware of the salt in my hair and my cheeks scrubbed red by so much air. My wife remarks on it. I tell her about the canal cruise. On safe ground, I talk too much. She sets down her knife and fork, folds her hands in her lap and listens.

'Out there I found there was too much sky,' I say. 'And too much air. And each breath filled me full to bursting and all my words left me. I was briefly not me and not anyone. Empty and filled up both at once. And clean – afterwards I felt so clean. Cleaner than I have ever felt before. And new. That must be what baptism is, the being made clean and new.'

She lets me speak without interruption. Then, when I have exhausted all thought and there are no more words, she picks up her knife and fork again, leans a little towards me and asks if this is something to do with the book I am writing.

I think for a moment before replying.

'No, today was an escape from my writing. A drawing of breath.'

We do not then have anything more to say and so we continue with our dinner in silence.

Woman in Blue

vi

He loves me not. He did not come today. That happens. Most come only the once. I do not miss them when the gallery closes and it is dark and the mice run on tiptoes along the tops of the skirting boards. But with him it is a little different. He did not come today and I have grown used to him coming. He is expected and I look forward to his gaze. There is something in his looking, something childlike and clean. I miss that.

How many men can a woman love in a lifetime? How many if she is made into a painting and a lifetime stretches beyond the ordinary span?

He did not come today.

All men can be fickle, it seems. There was a day when Meneer Johannes Reijniersz was colder with me than before and the letter he had written for me that day had less in it. Not fewer words, but less talk of lying down with me or standing so close he could breathe in the scent of me – the sweet hot-milk smell of me mixed with the rosewater. The change had, I think, something to do with his wife.

Catharina had been in his studio after our session the day before. That's what he had written in this latest letter. She'd been looking for a white faience jug with a pewter lid that she knew Meneer Johannes Reijniersz had used in previous paintings. That was her excuse, at least. She found that day's letter torn into a hundred pieces and she found bits of words taken all out of context, words like *love* and *whispers* and *kisses* – he had written something about my lips and how in truth when they moved through the words of his letter it was as though I was speaking kisses to him.

He discovered his wife weeping over the painting.

'She is so pretty,' she said.

'All girls are pretty in their own way,' Johannes had said. 'It is something to do with the light.' (I only called him Johannes when he was not near enough to hear me, saying it with only breath in the name so it was like something said to only God.)

'It is not that,' said his wife.

'No? Then what is it?' he said.

'You think I cannot see it in what you have painted? You think it is something hidden? The yearning. The weight of that yearning. It is what has come between us, my husband. It is why you do not reach for me when we are alone in the dark together. Why all the warmth has gone from your words when you speak to me. There is a distance that is come into our bed – the opposite of what is in your painting of her.'

'It is just a painting,' he said feebly – something said can be truth and a lie both at the same time. Meneer Johannes Reijniersz understood that. 'Another month and it will be finished, and before God she will be nothing more than a woman praying in church who I once saw, someone I thought a fit enough model for a painting; a month more and the painting will be sold.'

I pitied him for his 'before God'. That would damn him when nothing else that had passed between us would.

Maybe he took his weeping wife into his arms then – he did not say that in the letter but it is something that husbands do. And maybe he held her close enough she could believe in their love once again.

I told Katrijn about the wife looking for the faience jug with the pewter lid, but I did not say more than this; that way I can swear to Heaven that I told truth, but God and I know that this truth feels as heavy as a lie.

'And is the painting not yet finished?' Katrijn said.

'Not nearly finished,' I said.

She was quiet then and closed into herself. And maybe I was too.

At the house of Meneer Johannes Reijniersz, as I was leaving after the morning's session, I discovered one of the words from the letter that the wife had found in pieces. It was lying on the stairs and just in the light where it could not easily be missed – I think it must have been placed rather than fallen. And the word, written in his hand, in the hand of Meneer Johannes Reijniersz, was *truth*. I did not know what she meant by leaving this for me to find.

And, when all is said and done, what is truth? I do not think she knows and I do not think Meneer Johannes Reijniersz does either.

He loves me not.

A Man in Amsterdam

vii

I think of the painting as an invitation. It draws me in, like it is a whole world of its own, separate from this world, which can be entered only through the painting. It's not just me who feels this. I have seen others who are similarly affected by the Woman in Blue. They lean into the painting, lean into her, looking for the trick in the artist's brushstrokes, not quite believing their eyes.

One woman I saw looked as though she was going to step into the painting – she stood on her tallest tiptoes and I thought she was suddenly without weight and that she might rise up off the floor; the look on her face was the look of the saints in ecstasy. A little like Bernini's Saint Teresa – not the collapsing and limp swooning body of the white marble saint but just the look on her face, eyes half closed, mouth slack and open as though marble might breathe, and the light on her falling from above, white and pure. There is a sculpted angel beside Bernini's Saint Teresa, holding a spear in one hand.

The woman saw me watching her and turned to explain.

She had come to Amsterdam just to see the painting, she said. It was like a pilgrimage. She had seen it once before, when she was a child. Her father had brought her to see it. She said that when she was with him for that first visit, she thought her father was in love with the woman in the painting.

'It was in the way he looked at her,' she explained. 'I didn't understand it before, but I think I do now. Maybe I am looking at her the same way my father did. Maybe I am a little in love with her now, as he was then. Is that silly of me?' she said.

And there it was. Something new in the painting. Something I had not thought about before. It was alright for this woman to love the Woman in Blue and for any or everyone in the gallery to feel the same. I felt no sense of jealousy, felt only something more generous and open, for the Woman in Blue that they saw was not the same Woman in Blue that I saw. Yes, it was the same painting, but it was different too.

'I have given her a name,' I said to the woman without looking directly at her. 'I call her Lieke. I don't know why.'

The woman in the gallery took my hand in hers and together we looked at the *Woman in Blue Reading a Letter*. There were no words then. And time stopped or ran away without us noticing. Maybe the bells of the Nieuwe Kerk rang out the hour. And people behind us tutted, wanting us to move on so they could hold their own holy communion with the Woman in Blue.

When the woman in the gallery was done looking, she let go of my hand and walked quietly away.

I have looked it up and Lieke *is* a real name. It is the Dutch diminutive of Angelieke, which means 'angelic' or 'angel-like'. I do not know how the name came into my head, but it feels right, and so I call the Woman in Blue 'Lieke' from now on. And thinking that somehow brings me closer to her, to the Woman in Blue; I can't really explain it beyond that. I write something of this down in my notebook.

I do not ask my wife about her work, not above the general enquiry as to how was her day. Her reply, when it is in words and is not simply a shrug of her shoulders or a dismissive wave of her hand, does not invite further interest. She does not ask after my day, and I am fine with that and fine with not knowing about hers. She sees I am writing but she knows not to ask – not yet anyway.

Ideas, writers' ideas at least, are so fragile sometimes and so without shape that they are not something that can easily be held in the hands. If they are talked about before they are written then there is the risk that they will thereafter be broken and not have so many words in them. Writing is sometimes a search for meaning, and if the idea has already been talked about then the meaning has been found and so the search is no longer urgent or even necessary. And so we writers do not talk about what we are writing about, or what we plan to write about. It is only after it is written that we talk.

Maybe it is the same for artists and their paintings.

Woman in Blue

vii

He loves me.

Even when he stands there holding the hand of another woman, he loves me. It is what I have come to expect, but despite that it always feels like something new when it happens. Love is like that, I think. He loves me and he does not know what to do with that love and so he comes here day after day.

Being there is important. Being present – nothing happens without that. Not even love. And in the end he will come to know what it is he must do.

The same is true for us all. For Meneer Johannes Reijniersz too.

One day, our session was interrupted by a visitor, a gentleman of means, one of Meneer Johannes Reijniersz's clients. He was dressed in rich velvets and brocades and he did not remove his hat but let it announce his wealth to the room. It was fashioned from the best beaver fur that came all the way from Canada. The brim of the hat was so wide the sun did not fall on him.

I kept my pose even though Johannes set aside his brushes. The gentleman was brought in to see the painting on the easel – not yet finished but still fine enough to be shown.

Douglas Bruton

There was a silence as the gentleman took in the subject of the painting. I think Johannes may have held his breath, waiting for the man's response. I know that I did. Then the gentleman patted Johannes heavily on the back and pronounced him a genius.

'Beyond doubt a bloody genius,' he said. 'And I love her. I love your Woman in Blue.'

This pleased Johannes. He could not hide the pleasure he felt at his friend's approval of the painting. It was written in the smile that he could not suppress and in the lightness of his step and in the stumbling of his words of thanks.

Then this man looked from the painting to take in the view the artist had. He approached me; not the chair nor the heavy unfurled bolt of dark cloth were any obstacle to him. He looked me up and down, glanced back over his shoulder at Johannes and winked. Men think when they do this that it is something unnoticed.

'You are a very lucky young woman,' the man said to me. 'To be painted by the great Vermeer is something indeed. You will live beyond one lifetime and beyond even two in the painting he makes of you.'

I may have smiled at this, forgetting in the moment my mother's admonition against giving such encouragement to men in rich clothes.

Then the man caught my chin in the cup of his hand. He held it not gently, not as you might hold a fond pet like a dog or a kitten, but firmly, as you might a horse that is sometimes wilful. And he leaned into me and kissed my cheek. His breath smelled of onions and his kiss was wet; I think I might have gagged. I don't think he noticed.

But I was not the only one to respond so negatively to this man's unlooked-for kiss. Meneer Johannes Reijniersz crinkled his nose and he looked away and he shuddered.

When the client was gone, he broke a brush in two with a sharp snap and threw the pieces to the floor. He said he was sorry, as though it was he himself who had transgressed.

'He is an unholy ass,' said Meneer Johannes Reijniersz, and it was the first and only time I ever heard him speak ill of anyone.

When I told Katrijn – out of earshot of my mother – she balled her fists and punched the air hard. She stamped her feet and sucked air into her cheeks and blew it out with force, like a cow when it is whipped with a hazel stick and must move from the warm barn into the cold green pasture. 'Gentlemen are not so gentle in their manners when they are around pretty women,' she said, all her words cat-hissed and spat. 'You should know this by now, Lieke!'

I laughed at that, at Katrijn sounding so like my mother.

She looked a little concerned and her brow lowered and knotted in disapproval of my laughter.

'Maybe this has all gone far enough and should go no further,' she said, her voice so quiet and urgent and pleading.

I was afterwards not so soft as feathers when I rubbed the wool grease into her hands, and I perhaps tied the cotton bandages a little tighter about her fingers. She moaned, but did not scold me to be softer.

'Gently,' said my mother from the other room.

But I was not gentle. I could see the pain I caused Katrijn by this and I did not straight away share that pain but only was something rougher with her chapped hands.

I said nothing more to Katrijn, nothing to soften what I had done or to soften what that man had done, not that night or the next silent morning, and perhaps Katrijn understood by this that there was no going back on the plan we had made together.

As for Meneer Johannes Reijniersz, with his condemnation of the man in the beaver-skin hat – well, Meneer Johannes Reijniersz loved me.

And it was fine for him to love me, and for anyone else to love me. At least, in a *painting* it was fine, in *his* painting – but loving me outside of the painting was, it seemed, something Johannes could not bear anyone but himself to do. That was something that stung Johannes, as though a dear friend – his friend – had stolen something from him when his back was turned, except his back was not turned and the thing stolen was taken right from under his nose and in full view and so this man in the beaver-skin hat could no longer be counted a friend.

He loves me.

A Man in Amsterdam

viii

'They talk about you,' says the man at the door to the Rijksmuseum. 'Every day you are here with your season ticket and you go to the one gallery in the museum. You always take the stairs. They say you can find your way blindfold. And it is the one picture you look at – Vermeer's *Woman in Blue Reading a Letter.* They say she has cast a spell on you and she will not let you go.' He laughs when he says this.

'Maybe you are writing an article on the painting and so you come each day to see if there is anything new to be said about her. Looking is such a complicated process. Most of the people coming here do not understand this. I think maybe you do. But you carry no notebook and all you do is look. Maybe you are not a writer but instead an international cat burglar with your eye on stealing her from us.'

He laughs when he says this also, but there is something unconvincing about his laughter.

'They watch you – do you know this? They have started making notes on your comings and goings. We have a diary for such things. One day you were with someone, a woman we have not seen before or since, and she held your hand, and so we think she might be your wife or an accomplice. She had an uncommon interest in the painting too. It was above an hour that you both stood just looking at our Woman in Blue.'

He does not say who 'they' are.

'Sometimes you sit on the low seat in the gallery, but always you are watching the Woman in Blue. They make a note of this too.'

I do not know why he is telling me all this, why he does not wish me a quick good morning as he usually does, opening the door to let me through.

'I have my own theory,' he says, his voice dropping to a whisper. 'I think you are married with children and you come here to escape. Plenty of men do that. Why, I have even done it myself of a Saturday, pretended I was working and had to come into the gallery, just to have an hour or two of peace and quiet. And our Woman in Blue is, I think, the quietest painting in the whole gallery.'

There is a pause. He has nothing more to say. Now it is my turn; he expects something from me in return. I shrug and smile weakly up at him.

'The truth is,' I say, but then I pause, not quite knowing what the truth is. I look over my shoulder in case there might be someone listening, then I lower my voice and speak as one sharing some secret confidence with the man at the door. Maybe I wink; I feel I should. 'The truth is I think I might be in love,' I say.

He laughs at first, as though he understands, as though what I said makes perfect sense. But as the words settle in his thinking or turn over and over like cartwheels, I can see the puzzle they leave him with.

'In love?' he says.

'Yes,' I reply.

'With our Woman in Blue?'

I shrug again as if to acknowledge that it is indeed a puzzle.

He waits for me to say something more. When nothing is forth-coming, he opens the door, stands back and lets me pass through.

I did not tell the man at the door of the Rijksmuseum that I am married, that I have a wife.

'And is your wife also enamoured of our *Woman in Blue Reading a Letter*? Is that why she came to the gallery that day, why she spent an hour just holding your hand and looking at Vermeer's painting?'

Then I would have had to tell him that the woman they had seen me holding hands with in the Gallery of Honour was not my wife but was someone else, someone I did not know, a stranger. Telling him that would only have muddied the water, and would not have changed materially the substance of what I said to him.

'The truth is I think I might be in love.'

'With your wife or not with your wife?' he might have said. 'With our Woman in Blue or not with our Woman in Blue?'

'Yes,' I'd have replied.

You see how much more complicated it could have become. And that's without him knowing anything about the fair-haired, blue-eyed girl I sometimes imagine I see in the painting of the Woman in Blue.

As for what I actually said to the doorman of the Rijksmuseum, 'The truth is I think I might be in love' – what does that even mean? In love with my quiet wife, with the Woman in Blue, with a blue-eyed girl whose hand I once held? With all of them at the same time maybe, but loving all of them differently? There must be something in that, something of meaning.

It is quiet in the Gallery of Honour. I stand in front of Vermeer's painting, breathing in and breathing out, each breath measured and slow. I take it all in, the whole of the painting. To think that something so beautiful was once just an idea in an artist's head and now it exists in the real world. My heart quickens. And it occurs to me then that each of us visiting the painting sees it differently – and when, afterwards, we think of the painting it is then an idea in our heads. And there is something in that idea I carry away with me that I love, as much as there is something I love in the painting I see before me. And so I say I love the Woman in Blue meaning my idea of her, just as I say I loved and still love a girl I once knew, the memory of her – her hair with sunlight in it and her eyes the colour of the sky – and just as I say I love my wife, even if I do not always put that into words.

Woman in Blue

viii

He loves me not, for it is not me he sees in the picture but Johannes's idea, something that existed in Johannes's head even before he saw me that day in the church. Seeing me, Johannes thought I might be the right shape for his idea, the right colour of hair, the right softness, the right complexion. He could already see me in the shop-bought blue bedjacket, could see me holding the letter in my hand. I think he might even have been able to paint the picture of me without me ever entering his studio, so fixed was the idea in his head.

So, this man who visits me every day, his heart beating fast like a skittery drum, he loves me not. He loves only Johannes's idea.

'When he kissed you, what was it like?' said Meneer Johannes Reijniersz.

The kiss was already a week old and still it troubled him.

'You do know that I did nothing to invite the kiss?' I said. 'That it was the same as something stolen, which is to say something taken that did not belong to him.'

'But what was it like?' he insisted.

He was looking to blame me for it. Men do that.

'If anything, it was your painting that was to blame. He fell in love with that before he turned his eyes upon me. Without your painting he would not have given me a second look. Maybe he wants to buy your painting and you can charge him overdear for it, which will be like charging him for that kiss.'

'I would sooner sell my painting to the devil himself,' said Johannes.

I snatched at the letter he had written for me, the letter I was to hold for that day's session. It was blotted and the paper was somewhat ruffled, as though it had been written in tears. And what was written was full of stings and cuts and pinches. He was not happy with how I looked when I read it.

'But the kiss,' he said again. 'How was it?'

I cleared my throat, as if to deliver a prepared speech in answer to his question, but I had nothing to say.

'Well?' he pressed.

I felt sorry for him then.

'It was a kiss. I am not an expert in men's kisses but I do think it was a little wetter than any woman would have liked. And his breath smelled sour, as though he had been eating onions or three-day-old fish. And he did not close his eyes, but stared into mine as though he knew what he was doing was an affront to decency. And his fingers gripped my chin so that I could not break away. He was no gentle man.'

Meneer Johannes Reijniersz nodded and bent his head over his paints and his brushes.

I was not finished.

'I should much rather gift a man a kiss than have one taken from me as he did,' I said. Then I dropped the pose, walked up to Meneer Johannes Reijniersz and waited for him to lift his head, which he avoided doing at first. When at last he did, I stroked his cheek with the warm flat of my palm and kissed his other cheek, soft and lingering. I had wanted to kiss his lips. It was, I think, the right time for this, but in the end I kissed only his cheek. That was in the way of a gift.

I did not wait to see his response but walked back to my place in his picture, picked up his sour letter and struck the pose again, knowing he would have to come to me to sort the folds in my skirts and the lie of my hair. He was laggardly in doing this.

When I told Katrijn about our exchange – and I was careful only to tell her so much and not to tell her about the kiss I had given Meneer Johannes Reijniersz – she said she thought my artist was jealous. She called him 'my' artist. She did not say that he loved me but said only that he was jealous, and jealous on account of the money he'd paid me. 'He thinks you belong to him, at least in the time he is paying you for.'

I shrugged and said perhaps she was right.

She said she was certain and that it was so with all gentlemen, and it was the same with the gentleman in whose house she worked.

Then she took my hand and, as though I was a young child and had something to learn, she told me a story.

One day there had been a delivery to the kitchen of the house, brought by a boy with skinned knees and fish scales pressed into the palms of his hands like silver stuivers. The boy said that the master of the house had asked for a whole salmon to be delivered to the kitchen – fresh and caught on the line was what the boy said. The salmon was wrapped in scrap linen and wrapped again in hessian. The boy held it as though he was a mother cradling an outsized child that she would rather put down. Katrijn had gestured for him to lay the fish on the scrubbed kitchen table, and she helped in the doing of this. He was, she said, a pretty boy underneath the dirt and the fish smell. She asked after his name. She then rewarded Luuk with a piece of cake, which he ate without sitting at the table. Before he left, Katrijn bent and kissed the boy on the cheek. It was nothing, she said, except that the master had chanced to come into the kitchen at that moment and he thought it was something. Even before the boy had closed the kitchen door and was gone, the master scolded Katrijn for what she'd done. Not for the gifting of the cake but more particularly for the kiss – something so small and of so little weight, but that kiss somehow belonged more to the master than the cake did.

'Your artist is without a doubt jealous to have had his property misused by your man in a beaver-skin hat.'

She let go of my hand then.

I did not mind that Katrijn called Meneer Johannes Reijniersz mine, but I resented that she thought the beaver-skin-hatted gentleman was also mine. And that Katrijn had reduced me to property, I resented that also – but maybe that was how Meneer Johannes Reijniersz saw me and that was all his jealousy really was.

He loves me not.

A Man in Amsterdam

ix

Dearest Lieke,

I do not know what this is, how a painting can have such power. At first I thought I must be mad, for this – whatever it is – has all the hallmarks of madness. But then love is the same and it has all the hallmarks of madness too.

And, like love, this all happened by chance. It was another painting I came to see and I was stopped in my tracks seeing you. That was when I bought the postcard. I thought it was nothing more than that. But one day I came back by myself and I did not tell anyone where I was going. Most particularly I did not tell my wife.

There is something in that, I think. And I am without my wedding ring most of the time I am with you and I know I said before that there should not be anything read into that, but now I am not so sure.

The man at the door – I confessed to him that I was in love – tries not to look at me in the morning now when he opens the door to me. And he only nods to me and does not have any good morning words. He thinks me mad, I think.

And now I am writing letters to you. The man at the door gave me the idea. He thought I might be writing an article about you for a magazine and he wondered why I did not have a notebook in which to record my observations. And so I have a notebook now and in its pages I write letters to you. That is a madness, surely.

'But no,' I hear you say, your voice soft as wind-blown dandelion clocks. 'Are you not a writer? Is this not just an idea you had that you are now putting into words? A story of sorts. One only you can write.'

On the table in the picture of you there is an open box. Like a small chest where a lady might keep those things she treasures above all else. Letters that are not dressmakers' bills or shoe sales receipts. Pressed faded flowers that were given to her by men soft in love – poppies and forget-me-nots and pansies. And small pieces of jewellery handed down from mother to daughter or received as love tokens wrapped in lace handkerchiefs. I see a small part of a pearl necklace on the table. (Pearls he paints with a subtle loveliness, and this is the only complaint I have about how he has painted your hair, for in the painting your hair conceals your ear and had it not he might have painted a wonderful pearl earring there.)

And I wonder what I might give you to remember me by. And I wonder if this letter – when it is done and I have passed it to you, dearest Lieke – will have a place in your box. Do you think it might? Or am I mad to even think this could happen?

*

I wrote the letter before my daily visit to the Rijksmuseum. I waited until my wife had left for work, then I stole out to find a quiet place where I could drink coffee and eat the best Dutch apple cake. I found a table in the café garden at Hortus Botanicus – Amsterdam's botanical garden near Wertheim Park on Plantage Middenlaan. The waitress who took my order said she was sure there were tables inside if I preferred. She said it was warmer inside. I shook my head and told her I was fine. I do not think she believed me; she was cold. 'Really,' I said. She left to make up my order.

The words of my letter were a little scratchy and did not quite sit on the faint blue lines of the paper; that was something to do with the chill of that day. I was particular in using a blue pen.

The waitress, when she returned with my coffee and apple cake, said again that it was warm inside and it would be alright to change my mind.

The apple cake was flavoured with cinnamon and the spice nipped at my tongue as much as the cold nipped my fingers.

Woman in Blue

ix

He loves me.

His letter does not say he loves me, at least not in quite so many words, but he writes of love and he writes of me all in the same breath – madly, excitedly. And his letter touches me so that I am now sorry for him and for his soft heart.

I would write back to him but he has not gifted me his name so I would be writing to no one. Besides, I do not know what it is I should say. That I am glad for his love, but he must know it lacks substance or is cast in the wrong direction? That he is so close to learning the lesson, but it is something he has to learn for himself and not something that can be taught? That I love him too – as I have loved a thousand other men and women who have spent time with me as he does? He thinks he is the first, the only. All men think that, want it to be so. The truth is altogether different.

My mother always said silence is the best reply when anything else would only cause hurt. And so I am silent on the matter of his letter and his love. It is something he liked in me before.

Meneer Johannes Reijniersz's daughter answered the door when I called again, though in truth she opened the door even before my hand lifted to ring the bell. Her name was Maria. She told me that when I first called. She said she was sorry but her father, the artist, was not at home that day. She said he had been called away on business and she handed me a note, the paper warm and softened from the too-tight hold the girl had kept on it.

She said I was to call again the next day and she pressed into my hand two silver stuivers – just as her father had done every other day as payment for the morning's session. Then she quietly closed the door, so quietly that I thought she was keeping something from someone inside. Maybe her father had told her that the mother was not to know what she did.

I pocketed the money and the note and went to Delft's Nieuwe Kerk instead of home.

There was music playing in the church and somewhere a young boy was singing and his voice was like the voice of a girl or an angel – or so I imagined an angel's voice was. I sat near the back and I hoped not to be seen. I took out the note that Maria had passed to me and unfolded the paper.

Dearest Angelieke,

The painting is almost done. Two days more I think will be enough to see it finished. Then I do not know what. Sometimes when I am at the end of a painting I am briefly lifted up and filled with a sense of God's goodness; sometimes the picture is not so good as it could be, not so good as it was in my head when I started, and then I am cast down and am poor company until another painting takes up my attention. But this time is something different, for it is more than the painting. Let us say it will take a week to complete and that will give us a little longer together.

Today I was pulled away from you on some guild matter. It is a thing of so little importance when set next to the painting, but it is a duty I could not pass by.

As to the 'gift' you made to me when last you were in the studio – I do not think I said to you then what it meant to me. I was still something mad by what had happened before with the ungentle gentleman, whose name is a bad taste in my mouth even yet. It is enough, I hope, to say that your gift to me left me feeling blessed or touched by God. I do not think it is too much to say that.

Respectfully,

Meneer Johannes Reijniersz

He was a man in a position of some standing in Delft, a married man and a rising star in the town, and so I understood that he had to be careful with his words and did not flinch at his 'respectfully'. And though I did not know what should be done with what he had written, of one thing I was certain: he loved me.

I left the church and walked down by the river Maas. The air there smelled washed clean. I read what he had written again and again, until I had all his words by heart. Then I tore the paper into a hundred pieces – it was what he would have wished me to do – and I flung the pieces onto the surface of the water for scattered ducks to peck at.

My mother was surprised to see me home so early in the day. She was bent over a piece of lace she was in the process of finishing, all the coloured bobbins dancing and clicking in her fingers and the threads slowly spinning until they were pinned down like lovely spiderwebs against a black velvet cloth. She thought something must have happened, that maybe I had crossed Meneer Johannes Reijniersz in some small way and he had ended the contract we had. Perhaps she knew about the money I kept under my pillow and she feared there would be no more.

I put a pan of milk onto the stove so that we might have the treat of a hot drink curdled with ale and flavoured with rough sugar and cinnamon. I assured my mother that I had not upset Meneer Johannes Reijniersz in any way whatsoever.

Then she assumed that the gentleman had transgressed in some shape or form – a hand laid on my breast, perhaps, or my skirts lifted above my knee, or worse. I laughed when she said this and I said she was not to be concerned and that Meneer Johannes Reijniersz had simply been pulled away on guild business. Nothing more than that.

I did not tell my mother about the letter – his letter – torn to pieces and tossed onto the gentle running water of the river Maas. Nor did I tell Katrijn when she came in from her work and my mother couldn't wait for her to take her dinner but launched into the story of my being home for the whole day and Meneer Johannes Reijniersz only away on guild business. Katrijn looked at me sideways at that. Maybe she suspected something more was in the story of my day being empty and myself not a stuiver poorer for the day being mine and not his. I'd bought Katrijn some sweet biscuits and had set them out in a neat arrangement on a small plate for her coming home; this did not banish her suspicions but only heightened them.

And Katrijn thinking there was something more in my being paid for my empty day gave me to consider that maybe she was right and maybe Meneer Johannes Reijniersz did not think of me as property – a thought I'd had previously – but rather held me in some greater regard.

He loves me.

A Man in Amsterdam

x

What colour are her eyes? That we can only guess at. I imagine they must be blue. That would be in keeping with the painting, I think. Yes, blue, and perhaps flecks of gold adrift in the blue. I have known eyes like that; the same girl who once poetically tucked her light brown hair behind her ear had such eyes.

It has occurred to me before now that maybe this girl is the reason that the painting holds me captive as it does. Indeed, when I look again I see there is enough in the painting that it could be her, with the hair done a little differently and dressed up in clothes she never wore, heavier clothes that thicken the shape of her. And when I say that I love the Woman in Blue, maybe what I am really saying is that I love this girl even when she is a girl no longer and is only so in memory.

But then the thought of her, this gold-flecked-blue-eyed girl who, with the simple drag and draw of her index finger, wrote something that was close in memory to poetry – the thought of her came after and was not a part of my first response to the painting, and so things don't add up.

They must be two different things, and yet they feel joined together.

Of course, it is also the case that the Woman in Blue might be no woman at all. That is to say, she might be nothing more than a figment of the artist's imagination, an idealised picture of a seventeenth-century woman. Who's to say she is anything more than this? The almost photographic quality of the painting deceives us into thinking she must be something real, someone real. That can happen.

Or maybe she *is* someone real, but the artist has added something to his painting of her, made her a little more perfect than she ever was. That happens too. Maybe she was a little more stooped or her hair was not so neat or her lips not so perfectly kissable. I read somewhere that in Vermeer's *View of Delft* he shifted the buildings a little to suit his compositional needs; he could just as easily have done some 'shifting' in his painting of the Woman in Blue. We already know that he painted the jacket with a fur-trimmed hem and then changed his mind and removed it.

I may also have read somewhere that the map once took up more space on the back wall than it now does, that Vermeer later changed this to improve his composition. I have tried to find the place where I read this, but it eludes me and so there is every chance that I misremember it.

Memory does that. My memory of the girl I once loved who is somehow both in this painting and not in it, well, that memory is all shop-bought and new and not like something slept in and crumpled; it is something perfected by the distance I am from her.

'What colour are your eyes? Tell me.'

I am alone in the gallery, alone with the Woman in Blue, and for the first time I speak my thoughts out loud. I want to interrupt the reading of her letter, even if it is my letter, just for the briefest moment. Just long enough for her to lift her head and look back at me – a scold-look, perhaps, but a look held long enough for me to see the colour of her eyes.

'Are they blue?'

Of course, I am being fanciful here. I do not say my thoughts out loud for I am never completely alone in the Gallery of Honour; there is always a guard lurking nearby, waiting for me to lean in too close to the Woman in Blue, making a small note of the time I spend with her, and of the expression on my face, what it says to him.

I sit on the low seat and take my notebook from my jacket pocket. I write down everything I have just thought – all the stuff about what the artist might have added in his painting of the Woman in Blue, what he might have left out or 'shifted', and how she might be something invented rather than real. *Are her eyes blue?* I write that down too and I do not write an answer.

I try to catch all my fleeting thoughts, to put them down in words. But then it occurs to me that thoughts pinned down in this way change their nature and are a different fish altogether. Thoughts put into words behave differently and are not like thoughts at all but are something more certain and something more fixed. My thoughts here have become story.

I do not at this stage know where this is leading me, what it is that I am moving towards. Sometimes it feels as though I am pushing the whole story forwards; sometimes it feels as though I am being pulled along, being led towards something – a door, perhaps, one I am to open and to go through, and behind which is a discovery to be made, something that has meaning.

Hasn't the Woman in Blue said as much: that there is something for me to learn and that this – all of this – is simply a journey towards understanding?

Woman in Blue

x

He loves me not.

He loves a girl with blue eyes and mine are brown, a light brown, the colour of sand when it is wet with sea-salt tears or rain. He thinks it cannot be me that he loves, and that the painting of me is somehow a lie, that Meneer Johannes Reijniersz has painted me not as I am but as I would be if I were perfect.

'I want you just as you are, with your hair up – which I know is not how you ordinarily wear your hair. And dressed in a blue bedjacket, which is not something you wear. And reading a fake letter of love that leaves you just ever-so-slightly breathless.' That is what Johannes said to me at the start. What is important is Meneer Johannes Reijniersz's 'just as you are'.

Besides, how honest can a painting be when it tries to catch a moment, to still time to something frozen? This moment, the moment of the painting, is something that in reality stretched over months. An *ogenblik*, a blink of the eye – that is the lie if a lie is to be found. Time pressed into the smallest space, like an over-stuffed bag packed for a long journey. A hundred Nieuwe Kerk chiming hours pressed into a single moment. A counterfeit truth.

The light in that last week we were together in his studio was so different from the light in the first week. The seasons had shifted and each day the sun was placed in a different relation to the earth – further off. Meneer Johannes Reijniersz had to bring a foot warmer into the studio for that final week, and our sittings grew shorter and shorter. I wore warm woollen stockings and a second petticoat under the skirt and a thicker bodice under the blue bedjacket.

But there is another sense in which the painting is a lie, and all paintings fail in the same regard: there is none of the animation of the living in what he has painted. This is something I have seen in the dead, too, even those familiar to me and fond. My grandmother when she passed was laid out on the bed in her house dressed in her Sunday clothes and at first I thought it was as though she only slept, but when she did not move, not any part of her, not in the face or the hands or in any other portion, then I had the sense that this could not be my grandmother, for there was something vital missing – no breath or heartbeat; no thought or feeling. All of that is what is absent in a painting, the animation of the living, and so it is like me and not like me.

So what does it matter if he has brushed my hair a little prettier than it was, perfected the grace in my fingers holding the letter, straightened my back a little? It is a perfect lie or an imperfect truth. But I will contest that it is still me and no one else.

We buried my grandmother two years ago and on each anniversary of her death we knelt before her grave and spoke our thoughts aloud to her, telling her how things had been over the past year. Beneath our feet she was but ashes and dust and bones – but it was still the grave of my grandmother.

I expected Meneer Johannes Reijniersz to be closer on the day following my receipt of the letter his daughter had handed to me at the door. I expected warmth – more than can be supplied by a simple wooden foot warmer that was placed so near I could feel the air move under my skirt. But if anything he was a little further off, like the sun, as though the words he had written, words I had thrown like bread to the ducks on the river Maas, were nothing more than a perfect lie or an imperfect truth.

'Do you think you could give me blue eyes in the painting,' I said to Johannes when his back was turned, 'flecked a little with gold, like the sky with broken pieces of the sun adrift in the blue? Would that be too much to ask?'

He did not hear me, for the words had only shape and breath and no sound at all.

The morning flitted by in a moment. That's how it seemed. I am not sure I was really there. I held the pose the same as usual, but it was as though I somehow left my body and was not there and not anywhere. I wonder if that is what it is to be dead, like a great hole has been made in the material world and the hole so dark that if you peer in there is no bottom to be seen and all thought is lost in such a hole.

I did not even mark the Nieuwe Kerk bell tolling the hours.

Meneer Johannes Reijniersz said, when I was dressed in my own clothes again, that I had been a little restless and perhaps there was something that was in my head, something secret and unsettling.

For a moment I thought he knew more than he did. For a moment I thought he knew about the plan, though how he'd know I could not have said.

I was a little less myself when I was home again. My mother kept asking if the cat had got my tongue. She knew something was not right. She kept touching me, her hand on my cheek or lightly stroking my hair as she passed my chair, her fingers touching my knee.

'You are not you tonight,' she said.

She fussed over me as only a mother can and made remark on how cold my hands were and how pale I looked. My bedtime hot milk had a little spirit added to it and a little cinnamon and some sugar.

Perhaps Katrijn sensed it too, and she did not need me to tell her that the day had been full of holes. That night she waited until I had daubed wool grease over the cracks at her knuckles and into the creases of her palms – not so cracked or so creased as they were before, I observed – waited until after I had wrapped the soft clean cotton bandages about her fingers. The air in the house smelled of dry grass stored in wooden walled barns with sheep nestled in the straw giving suckle to new lambs. I might have said as much and in as many words – and if I did, that was more than I'd said all evening and in consequence my voice was a little undressed and shivery. Then Katrijn took me into her arms, held me tight as fists, and stroked the rosewater-scented back of my neck.

'And the plan?' she said. 'Are we still following the plan?'

I did not make any reply to that but let myself be held, all the way to morning.

A Man in Amsterdam

xi

'Where do you go all day?' my wife asked. 'Smelling so clean and with your shoes polished like mirrors. If I didn't know you better, I'd say you were meeting a woman.'

And that got me thinking about how much we really know someone, even someone we have spent our lives with, or the better part of our lives with, if by 'better' is meant something about the number of years and not just the quality of those years.

Thoughts are not words but something else entirely, and they are imperfectly shared if they become words. And how many thoughts might a man have in a single day? Too many to ever be written down. And what do these unwritten, unshared thoughts say of a man? And if they are not shared then what role do they play in defining who he is – who I am?

A part of me wants to tell her about the painting in the Rijksmuseum and the quiet that enfolds me when I am looking at the Woman in Blue. I also want to tell her about the girl with blue eyes whose hand I once held and how the movement of her index finger when she dragged her hair behind one ear was something that entranced me. I want to tell her about the man at the door of the gallery and his theory of why I have a season ticket but only go there to see the one painting.

She thinks the painting – *Woman in Blue Reading a Letter* – is Vermeer's sexiest and so I think telling her about my daily visits to the painting would be misunderstood.

'I am writing something,' I tell her.

Writers are funny about ideas, their own ideas. They are guarded, superstitiously against sharing them until they are fully worked out and set down on paper. My wife knows not to ask me about what I am writing.

'You shave and wear a clean shirt and clean socks to sit in a coffee shop and write?'

I shrug and that way there is no truth or lie in what I have told her. At least there is no hurt.

The Woman in Blue looks a little different each time I see her. Like something known and yet still like something new. I sit on the low seat and open my notebook. I make a small note on the picture, something about the blue in the shadows. I have seen this in Impressionist paintings by Monet and others, but not in any other Dutch painting from the seventeenth century. Rembrandt's shadows are all coffee grounds and coal.

The Impressionists understood something about the science of light and colour theory; Vermeer did not – he just understood how to look, to really look. Next door to Vermeer's house lived a Jesuit who was interested in ways of looking. He owned a camera obscura – an arrangement of lenses and mirrors that was an effective aid to looking. It is only speculation but is not too great a leap to say that Vermeer must have made use of such a device – not in the process of painting but in the act of looking. In this way he would have seen that in yellow light the shadows cast have blue in them and not black or brown.

And there are double shadows in the painting of the Woman in Blue. You can see it with the shadow thrown onto the wall by one of the chairs, the same with the rod at the bottom of the map. Strangely, the Woman in Blue herself casts no shadow; the wall where her shadow should fall is blank. When I notice this, the Woman in Blue appears to shimmer – like air above a hot road that seems to have the substance of water and ripples so the world looks like nothing more than its own reflection cast adrift on the river Maas.

'Are you real?' I say, bolder today than yesterday and careless of the people sitting beside me on the low seat. 'Or are you meant to be angel-like, and is the letter you hold not something you have received but rather something you have written and are keeping until the time is right to send it? Angels are messengers, after all.'

Of course, she does not look up from what she is reading – she never does – and so I am left alone with my thoughts.

At some point in the afternoon I become conscious that I am not alone, that someone is sitting beside me on the low seat in the Gallery of Honour at the Rijksmuseum. It is a woman and she is sitting so close to me I can feel the warmth of her leg touching mine. I am also aware that she is looking over my shoulder, reading the words I have written in my notebook. I am at first not sure how I feel about this – conflicted at the very least. Writers write to be read, after all; but then this is just a working out of my ideas and I am not yet sure it is intended for a readership.

'Interesting,' she says, this woman I don't know, and with her 'interesting' she stands and leaves without any further utterance. I have not looked at this woman, have only had an awareness of her – the warm press of her leg against mine, the sense of being read, and that one word she said, whispered into my ear so I think I am the only one who heard her: 'Interesting.'

But then there's something in this that leads me to something else, another thought, and I understand then that the Woman in

Blue does not need to look up to know I am there, doesn't need to see me to know me. There are different levels of knowing and – because thoughts leap off almost of their own accord and leap in directions we do not expect them to – I understand then that love also has different levels. The love I have for the Woman in Blue and for the girl with fair hair and gold-flecked blue eyes and for my wife and for the woman who silently held my hand for an hour standing in front of Vermeer's painting – the love I have for all these women (and who knows what other people might be included here) is different in every case.

I write all this down too and I can feel the Woman in Blue reading what I have written.

Woman in Blue

xi

He loves me.

'Angel-like,' he wrote; that made me laugh. Angelieke, angel-like. It is a game he is playing, I think, juggling thoughts and ideas. Shifting words around just as Meneer Johannes Reijniersz shifted the buildings in his celebrated painting of Delft, all to suit his compositional needs. And all that stuff he says about light and shadows – that is true and can be seen by a closer inspection of the painting.

Johannes one day explained it all to me. 'See,' he said, pointing to the shadow of a chair thrown onto the wall. 'There is colour in the shadow if you look, and the colour is blue.' He said it was obvious once you saw it. 'Shadows are not like black smoke or tea stains,' he said. 'They are sometimes blue.' And when he showed me, I could see exactly that.

As for my own shadow, which is not in the painting, he said that adding it would only cause an imbalance in the picture and that would distort the mood and the eye would shift out of the painting to the right and that was not the point. The point was to draw the viewer in.

'Intimacy is the point,' he said. 'Do you see?'

Johannes talked sometimes just to fill the space in the room, or sometimes to keep a distance between us. I don't know if he knew that.

'Do you think, Johannes...' It was the first time I had used his name to address him directly and it felt somehow lumpy in my mouth. 'Do you think you might hold my hand a while? For I am a little shaken today and I cannot explain why.'

He did not need to be asked twice – which is something that is said when a man is eager. It was as though holding my hand was something he had long wanted to do and which he had given up all hope of ever doing.

Where's the harm in holding hands, I thought. Before God and with no shame.

His touch was cold at first and I think mine must have been too. But together, his hand holding mine, we created a shared warmth. And an intimacy.

'Do you think that colours have their own temperatures?' he said.

I wanted to tell him 'hush' and for him just to be. Instead, I told him that I had seen his painting of *The Procuress* and that it was a picture that made me smile. And I said that I thought it was a painting filled with warmth. Not heat exactly, not fire, but something like a summer day. I think he liked that.

'That's all down to the red and yellow – the red of summer-field poppies and that particular yellow, which is not the yellow of lemons but the yellow of sunflowers in full shout.'

I laughed at that.

'Blue, on the other hand, is such a cool colour,' he said. 'Not so much cold but something that is slow and easy and does not overexcite the eye in the same way as red or yellow. And so I think colours might have different temperatures or moods.'

As he talked, his fingers seemed to caress my own without him knowing what he was doing. And his words slowed and the sound of him talking was like the softly enthusiastic movement of water over small stones and also like quiet laughter let loose.

'Johannes,' I said, not as an opening to the saying of something more, nor even as a question, but just to perfect the saying of his name and perhaps to freeze the moment.

He turned to me, lifted one hand to my cheek and just held me like that.

I saw then that his eyes were blue – maybe I had noticed this before, but seeing them so close I thought the blue was something remarkable, and I wondered if that helped him see the world more clearly and to see it more blue than it was.

'Angelieke,' he said, and in his mouth my name had music in it. 'Angel-like,' he said.

'Angelieke, pass me the flour,' my mother said to me. She was preparing to bake bread. It was a Monday, you see. It was early morning, but already Katrijn had left for work. I was not expected at Meneer Johannes Reijniersz's until the day had brightened and outside I could see it was still dark. I had fed the stove with logs so that the kitchen was warm in spite of the cold knocking at the door; the kitchen was warm every Monday, hand-in-gloves warm. Mother would bake three loaves of bread today, enough for the rest of the week, and so the kitchen was only warm like this on a Monday.

'Angelieke,' she said again, 'the flour.'

I passed her the bag of flour.

My mother has a way of saying my name that I only just now notice. It has scold and Sunday church and milk from the breast in it, which is to say it is filled up with love – a mother's love. And it is different from how Katrijn says it and different from how Meneer Johannes Reijniersz said it the last day I was in the studio.

'Angelieke – angel-like.'

So many ways to say my name, to say any name – and so many ways to love.

He loves me.

A Man in Amsterdam

xii

Is it a betrayal to love more than one person at a time, and then to keep it held back, hidden, so it does not cause hurt in the world?

'It is only a painting,' the Woman in Blue says, her voice suddenly in my world as mine has been in hers; at least in my head she says it, a thought that is both hers and mine. 'An arrangement of pigment, which is nothing more than stones ground down to softness and mixed with fine filtered oil, brushed onto canvas and fixed.'

'Not just a painting but also a memory,' I say. 'A memory of a girl I once knew and who must be old now, grey in her hair and her blue eyes a little less blue than they were.'

'A memory is just a thought,' she says, 'nothing much more than that. And a man – or woman – will have a thousand thoughts in an hour and some of those thoughts are fleeting contradictions of who we are and come from who knows where; I do not think a person ever can be judged on what passes through their heads.'

But the thought of this girl is not something fleeting. It is something I return to again and again. You see, I loved this girl with the gold-flecked blue eyes and the flick of her finger when she tucked her hair behind her ear; I do not think I ever told her I loved her, nor ever kissed her, though I seem to remember I held her hand once, but because I no longer trust my memory that might just be something I think I did. And this girl was my first love – fleeting and never forgotten, brief time expanded to fill years.

And maybe there are a dozen more loves like that in a life that is lived, and when a man grows old and looks back at the years he has had, searches through them for meaning, then it is only natural that he feels again the love for these women and it is only right that the feeling should be free from guilt. And without him knowing it, the love he relives turns into something else, something broader with widespread wings that reach out to embrace the whole sky. A universal love, if you like. Is that too fanciful? And it shows itself in everything the man says and does and it becomes a kindness that he performs every day or a gentleness that he demonstrates. He treads a little more lightly on the earth then.

So why does it sometimes feel like a betrayal to love like this?

Maybe the Woman in Blue is reading an old letter, for when I look at the sheet of paper she holds in her hands it is not so white as her underslip that we see above the open neck of her blue bedjacket. The paper is a light ochre, and so it looks like old paper, like a letter that she has kept for some time, folded and unfolded over and over again. A memory that she brings into the sunlight from time to time, a memory she revisits when the fancy takes her and when she reads what is written there.

Maybe the box on the table has a lock and a key. On closer inspection – not so close it might attract the attention of the gallery attendant – there looks to be a trailing blue ribbon on the table beside the pearls. I know that ladies do sometimes keep keys on such ribbons and the ribbon tied so it can be worn around the neck and the key kept hidden under her clothes and nearer to her heart. A box with a key would be needed to keep old memories secret.

And just the same, I keep locked away all my thoughts about the painting *Woman in Blue Reading a Letter*, and about a girl with gold-flecked blue eyes, and about the peace of being by myself in the Gallery of Honour at the Rijksmuseum. Or, if I am being honest, I write these thoughts down and that way I can say they are fiction and nothing more than that.

But then who is the Woman in Blue keeping her secret from?

My wife has put the blue Delft tile I bought her on the low table on her side of the bed, propped the blue tulips up as a balance to the postcard of Vermeer's *Woman in Blue Reading a Letter* on the table on my side of the bed.

'There was a time when tulips in Amsterdam were more precious than gold, and more expensive too,' I say.

My wife is beside me in the bed. She is reading and I have interrupted her.

'Tulip bulbs, that is. They were sold at great auctions. And each bulb carried a certificate of authenticity. Some were exchanged for more than a skilled craftsman could earn in a year – ten times more, even, as much as would buy a house on the Herengracht. It was sometime in the seventeenth century. When you think about it, they were buying and selling dreams, for there was no guarantee of what they had bought – a red-and-white-striped tulip called *Semper Augustus*, or something of a single colour like your blue tulips.'

My wife looks at the blue tulips on the Delft wall tile propped up on the table beside her.

'It was a fleeting fashion, this passion for tulip bulbs that overtook everyone and upended the economy, and when the humour had passed the market collapsed. Fortunes were made and lost to tulips.'

My wife does not know why I am telling her this. I am not sure myself.

'It was a passing madness,' I tell her.

'Yes,' she says. She waits for me to say more and when I do not she returns to her book.

'Like first love,' I say, or at least in my head I say it.

Woman in Blue

xii

He loves me not.

All his talk of betrayal and guilty secrets and locked boxes. Things have changed between us and he does not look at me but looks for keys on blue ribbons and judges the paper to be old and thinks that must be because it holds something long kept hidden, something that cannot be shared.

He is both nearer and further away. That's what it feels like. And so I think he does not love me today. This should give rise to tears and a feeling of something broken – the heart, maybe – and a feeling of loss, the same feeling that one has on hearing of the death of someone we once knew. But strangely I feel something else, something lighter, as though a weight has been lifted from my shoulders.

He is not there yet, not where he should be, but that does not worry me at all.

Johannes was also both nearer and further away – nearer to the end of our painting and so already further off, a distance that had to come between us when it was all over. He kissed me that day in his studio; I should have said that instead of leaving us sitting together holding hands in the cold blue light, his other hand to my cheek and the moment held. He kissed me, or I kissed him, and he closed his blue eyes and said my name quiet as prayer – Angelieke – and the kiss was lightly done and his lips soft and so I thought when we were alone together I should call him Johannes from then on.

But the following day, Johannes was different with me also.

I did not go behind the curtain to change and that was a statement of some sort. I undressed there where he could see me, if he only looked up from his mixing of paints and oils. I undressed and dressed again in front of him to let him see that there was no shame in what we had done.

After the kiss and while we were still holding hands, I had leaned into him, my head lightly resting on his shoulder, and we were quiet together for some time, church-quiet it felt like. Then I spoke – all the easier for not being able to see his face – and I told him I wanted nothing from him, that I knew who he was and I understood he was married and I did not want to break things but only to mend.

He did not take up his paints again that day, but the next morning he busied himself so much with the stirring and mixing that he gave me not the briefest look, did not see me undressed or dressed again in the blue bedjacket. He did not come to fix the pleats in the skirt or to arrange the hair on my cheek or to breathe in the scent of rosewater on the back of my neck. It was no matter, for those things in the painting were done. Indeed, I did not know why he was mixing so much paint, why we were going through the motions of posing and being quiet and still and blue, for we both knew the painting was finished and all we were doing was pretending so we could have those last days together.

'My wife's time is near,' he said without looking up, without breaking from the task of mixing paint. It was as though he was speaking to himself or to God. 'I need to finish this painting and be done with it,' he said.

Be done with me was what he meant. He felt guilt after the kiss. He thought he was the cause of it and did not see that I had brought it all about. It was nothing of substance yet – a kiss and the holding of hands and the lying down together as children do when they are playing at grown-ups and playing at being married, that was all. He thought because it all began with the idea, his idea, that he was to blame for everything.

I should have felt something breaking – like a wine glass when it is dropped on a hard floor. I should have felt the loss, even before the thing I had was quite lost. Endings must sometimes be mourned, but I felt nothing. Not at that time, for even if he did not know it, we were not done.

Katrijn also knew that our plan was not yet finished. She wanted to know how it would be when it was all over, when the painting was finished and Meneer Johannes Reijniersz was no longer a part of my day – the bigger part of my day, she meant, for she thought I would still see him in the street sometimes or in church. 'How will you feel when it is done?' she said.

It was a test of sorts, Katrijn asking that.

We were sitting at the table in the kitchen. My mother was not in the house; she had finished her scrap of lace and had gone to make delivery of it to a woman in a grand house near Prins Hendrikkade. It would be a collar to a cotton blouse. I had taken the handkerchief out from under my pillow and laid it on the table; with some ceremony I peeled back the four corners of the handkerchief to reveal the money inside.

Katrijn began counting the money, stacking the coins into neat and regular towers. She left her question hanging in the air between us. I left it too, until she had finished counting.

'There was a day when I did not know the name of Meneer Johannes Reijniersz. A day when he was nothing to me and I was nothing to him. When the painting is finished, it will be like that day again.'

I do not think Katrijn trusted those words. I do not know if I did.

We sat in silence then, surveying the money that Katrijn had counted. It was almost enough.

'And there was a day when Meneer Johannes Reijniersz did not know the name of a woman called Angelieke, and when we are done it will be the same for him and I will be nothing to him. Already I have felt the distance between us growing. Be assured, Katrijn, it is all a part of the plan.'

He loves me not, but we are not yet done.

A Man in Amsterdam

xiii

The Rijksmuseum gift shop has a small pocket-sized book about the painting *Woman in Blue Reading a Letter*. It is part of a series of books with each one focused on a different painting in some detail – *The Singel Bridge* by George Hendrik Breitner, *The Threatened Swan* by Jan Asselijn, *Children of the Sea* by Jozef Israëls. Some of the books are published in several languages – English and French and Italian. But for some reason the book about the Woman in Blue is published only in Dutch, and so she keeps her secrets close.

There are also notebooks for sale in the shop with a detail from Vermeer's painting on the cover, and bookmarks the same and mugs that are thick-lipped. You can even have a tea towel with the Woman in Blue on it; the blue on the tea towel is not so true as the blue in the painting, but it is only something for drying your dishes with and will no doubt fade to almost white after enough washes.

I think some people spend more time selecting these things in the gift shop than they spend standing in front of the paintings that they like. The same people take pictures on their phones of individual paintings – snapshots, taken in an 'ogenblik' – and I wonder how much they look at those pictures when they return home.

I have read something about Vermeer and perspective and how he sometimes used a pin and a length of twine to map out the lines and vanishing points in his pictures. He was not unique in this, but they have found pinholes in some of his canvases to verify it.

Standing in front of *Woman in Blue Reading a Letter* I try a small experiment. I draw an imaginary line from one top corner to the opposite bottom corner. I repeat this in my mind's eye with the other corners, trying to see where the two lines intersect. I have heard that this can be a useful exercise in determining the central point and therefore the central focus of the work.

It is hard to keep imaginary lines in your head and so I am not quite sure where they intersect. It could be that the centre of the painting is somewhere on her hands and the letter she holds. That's about as near as I can get standing in front of the painting.

'Never mind your imaginary lines and your picture centres and what the artist wanted you to focus on. You know what the subject of the painting is. By now you know. You also understand it is not necessary to know what the artist intended. You can decide what is important in the painting – what is important to you.'

That is the voice of the Woman in Blue intruding again on my thoughts. She sounds a little impatient.

'Just look, like you did at the start,' she says. 'See what I am, who I am. That is all that is required of you. Oh, and love, that is required also. Some days I think you are out of love with me and some days in. Do not be so fickle.'

I look over my shoulder, to left and to right, just in case I have said these things out loud, these things that are spoken by the Woman in Blue in my head.

'Look like you did the first time,' she says, 'or was it the second, when you fell head over heels. And you bought the postcard from the gift shop so you could carry me with you through the day, tucked into the pages of a notebook so the postcard did not become crumpled – except the corners became pinched and rounded and the surface of the card cracked like old paint. Look at me as you did then.'

So here I am, looking like the first time, and the blue pulls me in again but only so far. And her hands holding the letter that she reads catch a fleeting glance, but in the end it is her face that holds me fast. Her cheeks – are they ever so lightly flushed, grazed pink? I have seen women dressing for an occasion – a wedding or christening or a Christmas party – and just before leaving the house they check their hair and pinch their cheeks till they are pink. After a short time has passed the pinched-pink fades and the cheeks have only a memory of pink; that is what I think I see on the cheek of the Woman in Blue. Her eyes are downcast – please be blue – and her lips parted as though she is breathing in the words on the page she is reading.

Looking like the first time and remembering what it is to be in love all over again – with the Woman in Blue, with a girl with blue eyes and her hair tucked behind one ear and with my wife. I have neglected to say that my wife has blue eyes also, or that her hair was once fair and tucked behind one ear, and that I once saw her silently reading like the Woman in Blue with her lips parted as though she was saying the words out loud, and she sometimes pinches her cheeks pink before going out to dinner. And all of that is in the painting of the *Woman in Blue Reading a Letter.*

'It's about the painting in the Rijksmuseum,' I say.

My wife has asked me if I am almost finished with the writing project I have been working on. She has not asked to know what it is about, but I offer it up to her anyway.

'The *Woman in Blue Reading a Letter,*' I say, indicating the postcard on the table on my side of the bed.

'And has your piece of writing got blue tulips in it and a girl with blue eyes and apple cake?'

I look at her then, look at the blue in her eyes and the colour of her hair, a little grey in it now where once it had been the same colour as the woman in Vermeer's painting. The whole world suddenly tips a little and I have the sensation of falling – no, not quite falling, but a feeling of vertigo which is something akin to the feeling of doubt, a lack or a loss of certainty in what is and is not real.

'Blue tulips and a girl with blue eyes and apple cake – yes, it has all those things in it,' I say when I recover myself.

'Interesting,' she says.

Woman in Blue

xiii

He loves me. Don't you think he does, this man with the season ticket who comes to see me almost every day?

And all his talk of imaginary lines and centres of focus, well, he has quite missed the mark, but he will come to it in the end. I have confidence in that. After all, this is his story as much as it is mine – something we have shared.

The Nieuwe Kerk tolled the hour. It was already mid-morning and Johannes had not put paint on his brush. I did not think he would paint that day. And, having that thought, it felt like something I had decided for him. I held the pose for only a moment longer and then I dropped the letter onto the table. There were no words on the page; we were well past that and almost at the end.

Downstairs, the midwife had been called and we could hear a fuss being made in the kitchen and someone somewhere was telling Johannes's wife, Catharina, to just breathe. It was, as he had said, almost time.

I found the carpet we had lain down on before and I spread it on the floor. Then I added the cushions and I invited Johannes to lie down – as he had invited me back on that first day.

'It should end as it began,' I told him. What I did not say was that this was all a part of the plan.

Maybe he had expected this, for he lay down without a word.

Then I lay with him and I pulled his cloak over us like a blanket.

'Remember,' I said.

He did not hold me the same, had his back to me and thought to leave a space between us, for propriety. But he was no longer in charge and as I said before, we were not yet done. I slipped out of the skirt and the blue bedjacket and then I held him to me. Pressed myself to him. My lips to his ear, I said his name – Johannes – and for all I said it soft, it was something of a summons. He turned to face me. And I saw that his cheeks were wet with tears. I kissed him then, and I took his hand and put it under my slip and to my breast.

'I want nothing more from you than this,' I said to him.

On a cord around my neck I was wearing a small muslin bag of sweet-smelling herbs, henbane and mandrake, sea holly and bits of cinnamon bark – a love potion of sorts. The apothecary said together they would inflame a man's senses. I did not believe I had need of such cheap quackery, but then I thought, 'Where is the harm?'

I put my lips to his ear again. 'Nothing more from you than this,' I repeated.

As he entered me, I heard his wife downstairs cry out in her birth pains; beginnings and endings are sometimes so close they are almost the same thing.

'Breathe,' I said to him.

It was what he had wanted right from the start. It was what I had wanted also.

I shifted my hips a little beneath him. It was a form of encouragement. I'd read about it in a manual meant for new wives; it was something they were meant to do with their new husbands. He was a little clumsy at first but was not slow to respond; nor was he in a hurry, not to begin with. It was a gentle rocking of his body on mine, pressed together, pressed palm to palm like praying or like clapping where the hands do not quite separate but come together again and again. But then gradually the action took him over and he could not be held, like a horse when it bolts and it senses something like freedom and hurtles headlong towards it.

When he came, all in a hot and aching breathless rush, I heard his newborn take its first sudden breath. He collapsed and in that moment he heard it too, but he did not pull away and instead closed his ears to the sound, held me fast and near and said my name over and over.

'There, there,' I said to him. 'It is enough now.'

He loves me.

A Man in Amsterdam

xiv

I have bought a reproduction of the painting at the museum gift shop. It was not expensive. I have checked it against the painting hanging on the gallery wall just to make sure nothing has been cut from the picture, that the corners match up and are something true. The colours are a little altered in the reproduction but I can still see the faintest blush of pink on her cheek and the double blue shadows of the chair on the wall and the bright highlights on the almost hidden string of pearls.

When I am home, I lay the reproduction flat on a table in my study. Then I take a ruler and pencil and make my imaginary lines real, from one top corner of the reproduction to the opposite bottom corner. I do this on both sides so I can see just where the lines cross, just where the very centre of the painting is and where our focus should be.

The Woman in Blue is silent and as though she is holding her breath.

The lines cross not on the hands holding the letter as I had thought, but on a part of the blue bedjacket, just where her belly looks swollen. Indeed, I see now that the heavy fabric of the jacket does not conceal her shape but instead reveals it. And after all, the Woman in Blue *is* pregnant.

'And so we come a little nearer to the end,' says the Woman in Blue in my head.

I sit back in my chair. I breathe slow and deep. I had not expected this – had earlier rejected the idea. But now I feel she *must* be pregnant; at least, I cannot now just dismiss the idea. I do not immediately know what this means for my understanding of the painting. I have not discovered something new, something that has been missed by others, but somehow it feels new and right and the story of the picture has a completeness now.

Vermeer had a habit of recycling the props in his paintings. The white faience jug with the pewter lid is an example of this. And the chairs he uses are often the same chairs as appear in the *Woman in Blue Reading a Letter*. There is also a jacket that he is fond of, a yellow bedjacket trimmed with ermine. It features in no fewer than four of his paintings – one shows a lady seated at a table writing a letter; another has a seated lady interrupted by her maid who has brought her a newly delivered note. The blue bedjacket appears in only one of Vermeer's paintings.

Maybe the blue bedjacket was not his but belonged to his wife and it holds the shape of her when she was pregnant, the shape of her stretched and pressed into the fabric. I have seen well-used chairs that have held onto the shape of the sitter long after they have left the room. This would explain why the girl in the painting looks pregnant in the blue bedjacket and at the same time – with her delicate fingers – does not. The line between the Woman in Blue and Vermeer's pregnant wife suddenly blurs; somehow they are both in the painting at the same time.

Maybe Vermeer's wife re-staked her claim to the jacket once he was finished with the painting – they were not so rich that something so expensive could just be discarded – and perhaps this explains why Vermeer only used it in one of his paintings.

This does not change things. The Woman in Blue said I was a little nearer but still far off. Today I think I am almost there. She was talking about understanding and about love and memory and about something holy that is not limited to church or to God.

I feel lifted up. I can't explain it.

When my wife comes home from work, I take her hand and lead her into the study. I tell her about the picture and what I have discovered. I show her the lines and where they cross and I tell her the conclusions I have arrived at. I ask her if that is what she meant when she said it was Vermeer's sexiest picture.

She looks at me funny – almost as though she does not know me. 'Did I say that?' she says. 'I don't remember saying that.'

And maybe in the end she didn't say that or anything like it. And what began as a search for something hidden and sexy in Vermeer's painting has turned into something else, an altogether simpler story. Looking at *Woman in Blue Reading a Letter,* I have found there the shape of a girl I once knew and at the same time the shape of my wife and the shape of Angelieke – and I've found something about love and life and art in the painting too.

I hold my wife then and I kiss her and that feels right and perfect and true.

Woman in Blue

xiv

He lay heavy on me and was almost asleep when I shook him and said his name again – not Johannes that time, not as though we had just made love. 'Meneer Johannes Reijniersz, the Nieuwe Kerk bell is ringing. It is already midday and downstairs I think you are a father once again.'

I got up from the bed we had slept in, pulling my underclothes against my nakedness. It was what he would expect of me. I paused for a moment to take in the finished picture.

'Do you like it?' he said.

'I think I am pregnant,' I said to him.

He paled at that, his skin a little blue where the shadows fell.

'Pregnant?' he said.

'In the picture,' I said. 'You have painted me pregnant. That's what it looks like.'

The colour returned to his face.

He got up from the floor and adjusted his clothing.

'Not pregnant, but a little heavier than you are, perhaps,' he said.

I slipped behind the curtain and dressed in my own clothes.

'I have a buyer,' he said. 'For the painting. As soon as the paint is dry he will take delivery of it.'

'Then you will be done with me,' I said.

He made no reply to this.

When I came from behind the curtain again the door was ajar and he had departed the room. On the table he had left two silver guilders and a note to say that sometimes a painting is too quickly painted and he might have wished that this one had taken a little longer still. It was something written before I arrived for this morning's session. The ink on those words was dry. Underneath he had added just the one word: 'Love'. The ink on that was still wet.

I pocketed his note and the two guilders. I checked on myself in the picture one last time and then made my way down the stairs. There was too much going on in the house for my departure to be much noticed, except that when I got to the front door Maria was there; she must have been waiting for me. She took my hand and she looked up at me.

'Does my father love you?' Maria said.

'What makes you say that?' I asked.

'I have seen the way he looks at you in the painting when he thinks no one is watching. And he carries a handkerchief in his pocket and the handkerchief has been dabbed with rosewater and he sometimes holds it to his nose and breathes in – and that is your smell and so I think maybe he does love you.'

'He loves me, he loves me not,' I said to her. Then I kissed her cheek, let go of her hand and stepped out into the street.

Katrijn knew. She did not say it but I could feel that she knew even before I said anything. It was in the way that she unpinned my hair and let it fall over my neck – my never-more rosewater neck. She ran her fingers through the knots and tangles, combing the hair loose. She knew.

'It is done,' I said by way of announcement.

My mother looked up from her sewing. 'The painting?' she said. 'The painting is done?'

I nodded.

Katrijn held one hand over her mouth – catching her breath – and her other hand touched her heart. She must have known that I did not just mean the painting when I said it was done. She fussed over me, fetched a glass of cold milk for me to drink and a slice of apple cake that she had brought from the grand house. She pulled a small silver fork from her dress pocket – it was a fork from the grand house also.

'It is done,' she said, and when she said it the words were all breathless and blown.

Katrijn sat beside me at the table and we ate apple cake from a shared plate and a shared fork. I did not need to do a thing but eat. Katrijn did all that needed to be done, feeding me as she would an infant who had not yet learned the use of their hands. I sat with my hands nested in my lap and let myself be looked after.

'It is done,' she said again, as though she had to keep reminding herself of the fact. 'It is done.'

A Man in Amsterdam

xv

The man at the door to the Rijksmuseum sees me, but today he does not open the door for me.

'It is done,' I tell him.

'It is done?' he says.

'The thing I was writing,' I tell him. 'The piece on the *Woman in Blue Reading a Letter.* It is done.'

He smiles and I think I detect something like relief in his smile, and his shoulders relax so that he has a different shape to him, not so square but something a little more rounded.

'It is done,' he says, nodding.

He reaches for the door then and holds it open for me.

'This will be my last visit to the Rijksmuseum to see the Woman in Blue.'

'We do have other paintings,' the doorman says.

I laugh at that.

I take the stairs as I have done for weeks now. I approach her just as I have done before, spinning on my toes at the last moment, just when I am level with the painting. But today, somehow, everything feels different, as if she knows it is my last visit. She does not look up from the letter she is reading – she never has – but something in the painting tells me she knows. She is, it seems, more closed into herself, as if the moment Vermeer has given us in the painting is today more private and not anything to do with me.

I am alone with her, with the Woman in Blue. I stand square in front of her and lean into the painting. The attendant clears his throat to remind me he is there. He trusts I will not lean so far into the painting that I touch it.

'Pregnant?' I say.

She does not reply, nor did I expect her to.

Looking at the painting with this in my head it appears obvious. Then I am not alone.

'No, I don't think so,' says a woman beside me. 'At least, it is not certain. It is a bedjacket she wears and I think that can give a different shape to a woman. They were worn as an extra layer, and just so the woman was warm in her cold Amsterdam bedroom.'

'The room is in Delft,' I say to the woman standing beside me in front of the painting.

'It is cold in the bedrooms in Delft too, I shouldn't wonder.'

'If you draw two lines, corner to corner, where they cross is the centre of the picture and just where an as-yet-unborn child might be situated.'

'That is just maths,' says the woman. 'What do you actually see? What do you hear? What do you taste and smell? What do you feel?'

I couldn't hear anything – not coming from the picture. Not as I had before. 'I see a young woman, fair-haired and maybe her eyes are blue. She is quiet,' I say to the woman in the gallery with me. 'Everything's quiet.'

'Not even breath,' says the woman.

'I taste and smell lemons.'

'Something in the floor cleaner they use here,' she says.

'And I am wrongfooted, for she is at the same time both pregnant and not pregnant,' I say. 'Both are possible. When I came into the gallery I was more certain. But she is no longer speaking to me, you see.'

'But the matter of her pregnancy is of no importance, not in the picture, for it is enough that she is beautiful and the quiet that she has is something she brings to the viewer. A healing quiet, I like to think. Sometimes there's no need for words. Sometimes you just have to look and feel.'

I step back from the picture, look about me and find I am alone – except for the gallery attendant. I have only imagined a woman beside me, it seems.

'I feel love,' I say, not to anyone at all.

And if at the start we were not really talking, my wife and I, not in words at least, it does not mean anything. Sometimes words are all used up or cannot be relied upon or are not enough. There are other ways for couples to communicate with each other.

I tell my wife about the season ticket and about the man at the door of the Rijksmuseum and how this man knows me and each day wishes me a good morning and when I leave the museum at the end of the day waves me off with a '*goedenavond*' – good evening. I tell her about the day a woman held my hand for almost an hour as we looked at Vermeer's painting of the *Woman in Blue Reading a Letter*.

'I remember,' she says.

And the girl the woman in the painting reminds me of, I tell my wife about her too – though I do keep something back. 'She used to tuck her hair behind her ear, a simple catch and drag of one finger, done without any awareness of what she was doing. That's something you do when no one is looking,' I tell my wife.

She laughs when I say this and she takes my hand in hers. And so we are brought together in the end, which is, I think, what the Woman in Blue had planned for us all along.

And this, all of it, is just story, which is not to say it isn't also in some sense true.

Woman in Blue

xv

He loves me, he loves me not. Meneer Johannes Reijniersz and also the man with a season ticket to the Rijksmuseum in Amsterdam. He loves me, he loves me not; but it is no matter to me in the end, for *she* loves me and that is everything.

I moved away from Delft not long after the painting was completed. I left quietly so he would not notice me going. If he thinks of me now, perhaps I am only something he dreamed, for I no longer exist in his blue Delft world. He does not even have the painting – only a drawing he did one night by candlelight, though his daughter Maria had scribbled over the young woman on the paper, written all the words of Psalm 23 on the page, underlining some of the words and inserting some of her own.

I moved away from Delft to a village near the coast. It is no matter the name of the village, for I do not wish to be found. My mother came with me, and a young woman called Katrijn. And we conjured a story together that spoke sense to who people thought we were and at the same time hid what we really were – something about a husband, my husband, lost at sea, a bit sketchy on the detail.

I was already showing by this time – I was carrying Johannes's child just as I had planned, just as we'd planned. It was what I had wanted all along and what Katrijn had wanted too. She loves me, you see, and I love her and so we are as wife and wife and we sleep in the same secret bed. And now one day we will have a child together. It was the only way.

Katrijn lays one hand on the swollen hill of my belly, feels the baby shifting under her gentle caress. She leans in and kisses my belly, kisses the child inside. And her hands, Katrijn's hands, are not cracked but are soft like a lady's. She is learning lacemaking now from my mother and I am learning too.

And God – well, he has not struck me down yet, and if he is the God of love I think he is then he never will.

You see, I loved Johannes too. If I had not then I could not have done what I did. And I love a man in Amsterdam and a hundred other men besides and maybe even all men. And all women too. But I love Katrijn more than all those men and women put together, and this has all been for her and for the baby I carry.

The rest of my story is of no importance here and so on that I remain quiet. And if you want more of me I urge you instead to look at Johannes Vermeer's painting; it is about as near to me as it is possible to get. The painting is in the Rijksmuseum in Amsterdam. I urge you to go there and just look at *Woman in Blue Reading a Letter* and to have your own quiet dialogue with the Woman in Blue. She is always kind and so I think you will love her too.

And with that I think we are now done.

Postlude

He sometimes wishes he did not have to sell his pictures. He is not always sure the people he sells them to really look at them. You have to spend time with a painting to really see it. Just to have it hanging on a wall in a study is not really to see it. It has to be looked at in the right light also, and the viewer must be in the right frame of mind.

Word about the Woman in Blue Reading a Letter *leaked out before it was even finished and men at the guild approached him in the street eager to know if it was done. He already had a reputation in Delft and beyond. It was talked about in the baker's shop and even in church – though a church is not really the place for such gossip. The painting, when it was shown, only confirmed Johannes Vermeer's status.*

A report was written up in an Amsterdam periodical and passed around in the inns and courts of Amsterdam. The painting was described in plain language at first, but the writer of the article went on to say that looking at the woman in the painting it was almost as if she breathed – no, he said, correcting himself, nearer to the mark would be to say that the viewer felt his own breath stopped and he was somehow in the painting, on the threshold to the room where the woman stood. It was a remarkable work, the writer recorded.

And so the painting came to sell quickly and for a good price. Johannes had bills to settle and his family was one mouth bigger than it had been before he had started the painting. And when the Woman in Blue Reading a Letter was quite dry, Catharina parcelled it up, wrapped it first in paper, then in soft cotton and then in thick layers of hessian. The painting was placed in a wooden box made specifically for the transportation of the work. Vermeer never saw it again.

'You see,' he said to his wife. 'It is just as I said it would be. It is done and the woman is now not even a thought in my head.' And he took his wife in his arms and kissed her as he used to before and he laid one hand on her swollen breast and she did not make to remove his hand, not though her nipple was tender from the baby sucking.

'Not even a thought in my head now.' It was something he'd said several times since the day the painting had left his studio, and each time he said it Catharina doubted him more. He was not yet working on another painting; if he had started a new picture it might have gone some way to convincing her that the Woman in Blue was not so much in his head. But he was idle and listless and not attending to a husband's duties. Catharina some days discovered him alone in his studio, staring vacantly into the air. He said he was there for the quiet, or he was cleaning his brushes, or looking for his next painting, but his wife knew the truth was something else.

For hour upon hour Johannes sat at his empty easel and dreamed. Sometimes his attention was fixed on the absent painting and he even mixed fresh paint for the day's work, grinding the clay-like pieces of ochre or the brittle-hard lapis, eventually mixing the powdery pigment with fine oil until the right consistency was reached. Then, when he awoke to find there was no canvas on his easel, he scraped the prepared oil paint into a small spoon and tipped it into pig-bladder pouches that he tied tight closed and set aside in readiness for the next painting.

Sometimes he attended to the space that Angelieke had occupied in the room. His wife had cleared the table and rearranged the chairs, but Johannes could still picture it as it had been. He was even on one occasion observed fussing over Angelieke's imagined hair, standing close to where she'd stood before, breathing in the rosewater scent from her bared neck – it was Maria who watched her father do this and it was Maria who understood this panto-mime show of his love. She did not tell anyone what she saw, and particularly she did not tell her mother.

'He restoreth my soul,' she said, the words inaudible to all but God. She was quoting a line from Psalm 23 and it was what she wished for her quietly mad father, that his soul might be restored.

Some days Johannes walked out and he looked for Angelieke in the streets of the town and in the marketplace when it was busy. He made discreet enquiries as to where she might be found, but he had never known where she'd lived or what her family name was. And in church of a Sunday he looked for her – for Angelieke. Maria sat beside him some Sundays and she held his prayer palm in hers, stroking the back of his hand with her fingers. When he knelt to pray she heard him saying – quiet as breath – the name Angelieke, over and over.

The Woman in Blue was more than a thought in his head.

'It is always the way when he finishes a work,' said Catharina to her mother when she was explaining Johannes's absence at the dinner table. 'He is always then a little low and somewhat lost.

He once described it as being bereft when a picture is done and it is no longer a persistent thought in his head. We must be patient. He will return to us in due course.'

The children maintained an unusual quiet in the house, all except for the baby Johannes who cried almost without cease.

'Are you finished with the blue bedjacket?' his wife asked him one day. 'The nights are cold again and, husband, I should like to be warm in my bed tonight.' This was a comment on the distance Johannes still kept from Catharina when they slept together, as well as a ploy to take the Woman in Blue further from his thinking.

He went to his studio to fetch the blue bedjacket for his wife. When he picked it up from the back of the chair where Angelieke had left it, he held it to him, as though he was holding her. He wrapped the arms of the jacket across his shoulders and breathed in the smell of her, not the rosewater that she some days dabbed on the back of her neck and which had rubbed onto the cloth of the bedjacket, but the musty sweet and sour flesh smell of the woman that was Angelieke and that lay underneath the scent of rosewater, caught fast in the fibres of the jacket as well as in the threads of his memory. Johannes was disturbed from this reverie when Maria knocked on the door with a message from her mother, asking where on earth he could have got to with her blue bedjacket.

And that night his wife would have slept alone in their bed dressed in the bedjacket that smelled of Angelieke. Johannes excused himself and made a makeshift bed in his studio using the heavy Persian wool carpet to lie on with his own cloak drawn over him. Like that, he thought, he could imagine they were back at the start of things, or even at the breathless end.

But just as sleep overcame him, Johannes's wife crept in beside him, folded herself into his arms as the darkness filled all the *corners of the room. And Johannes dreamed of the Woman in Blue for the last time, dreamed he could feel Angelieke's warm breath on his cheek, could hear her softly whispering into the cup of his ear: 'Breathe.'*

Delft, late 1663

Acknowledgements

Thanks to Fairlight Books and their whole team for running with this wee book, and in particular to the very patient Sarah Shaw who helped so much to make this the book it is and Laura Shanahan for her careful copyedits. Thanks as always to the Demon Beaters of Lumb for their support. But mostly thanks to my wife, who took me to Amsterdam to see the Vermeer exhibition in May 2023; without that experience this book would not/could not have been written.

About the Author

Douglas Bruton is the author of five previous novels: *The Chess Piece Magician* (2009), *Mrs Winchester's Gun Club* (2019), *Blue Postcards* (2021), *With or Without Angels* (2022) and *Hope Never Knew Horizon* (2024). *Blue Postcards* was longlisted for the Walter Scott Prize for Historical Fiction 2021. His short fiction has appeared in various publications including *Northwords Now*, *New Writing Scotland*, *Aesthetica*, *The Fiction Desk* and the *Irish Literary Review*, and has won competitions including Fish and the Neil Gunn Prize. He lives in the Scottish Borders.

DOUGLAS BRUTON
With or Without Angels

'The thought in my head does not yet have shape or form, only direction, one picture leading into another.'

An ageing artist, faced with his own mortality, embarks on one final artwork. As he battles to complete the project, working with an enigmatic young photographer, he finds his past and present blurring. Through the act of creation and the memories it excavates, the artist comes to a realisation about what matters most, and what he will leave behind when he is gone.

This hybrid and innovative short novel responds through fiction to *The New World*, the final artwork by the late artist Alan Smith – which is in turn a response to an eighteenth-century fresco, Giandomenico Tiepolo's *Il Mondo Nuovo*. With sparkling, dreamlike prose, Bruton weaves a story around these artworks, arriving at both a profound exploration of the creative process and a timeless love story told in a new way.

'Experimental yet accessible, serious but playful, provocative but moving. Douglas Bruton is a writer of boundless invention'
—Stephen May, author of *Sell Us The Rope*

'A work of seriousness, empathy and beauty'
—*The Scotsman*

DOUGLAS BRUTON
Blue Postcards

Longlisted for the Walter Scott Prize for Historical Fiction 2022

Once there was a street in Paris and it was called the Street of Tailors. This was years back, in the blue mists of memory. Now it's the 1950s and Henri is the last tailor on the street. With meticulous precision he takes the measurements of men and notes them down in his leather-bound ledger. He draws on the cloth with a blue chalk, cuts the pieces and sews them together. When the suit is done, Henri adds a finishing touch: a blue Tekhelet thread hidden in the trousers somewhere, for luck. One day, the renowned French artist Yves Klein walks into the shop, and orders a suit.

Set in Paris, this atmospheric tale delicately intertwines three connected narratives and timelines, interspersed with observations of the colour blue. It is a meditation on truth and lies, memory and time and thought. It is a leap of the imagination, a leap into the void.

'It is a story, unlike our ability to see colour, that haunts and intensifies rather than diminishes with time'
—Carmen Marcus, author of How Saints Die

'I savoured every word of this beautiful novella and look forward to reading more of Bruton's work'
—Julie Corbin, author of A Lie For A Lie